ABOUT THE AUTHOR

Jana Fawaz Elhassan is an award-winning novelist and short story writer from Lebanon. She has worked as a journalist for leading newspapers and TV since 2008. In November 2015, she was featured in the BBC 100 Women Season, an annual two-week season that features inspiring women from around the world. Her first novel won Lebanon's Simon Hayek Award and her second and third novels (*Me, She, and the Other Woman* and *The Ninety-Ninth Floor*) were shortlisted for the International Prize for Arabic Fiction. This is her second novel to be translated into English.

ABOUT THE TRANSLATOR

Michelle Hartman is a professor of Arabic and francophone literature at McGill University in Montreal. She is the translator of several works from Arabic, including Radwa Ashour's memoir *The Journey*, Iman Humaydan's novels *Wild Mulberries* and *Other Lives*, Alexandra Chreiteh's novels *Always Coca Cola* and *Ali and His Russian Mother*, Shahla Ujayli's novels *A Sky So Close to Us* and *Summer with the Enemy* as well as Jana Elhassan's IPAF shortlisted novel *The Ninety-Ninth Floor*.

ALL THE WOMEN INSIDE ME

BY JANA FAWAZ ELHASSAN

TRANSLATED BY MICHELLE HARTMAN

Interlink Books

An imprint of Interlink Publishing Group, Inc.
Northampton, Massachusetts

First published in 2021 by

Interlink Books
An imprint of Interlink Publishing Group, Inc.
46 Crosby Street, Northampton, MA 01060
www.interlinkbooks.com

Originally published in Arabic in 2012 as *Ana Hiya wal Oukhrayaat* by Arab Scientific
Publishers, Inc., Beirut, Lebanon

Library of Congress Cataloging-in-Publication Data
Names: Hasan, Janá Fawwāz, author. | Hartman, Michelle, translator.
Title: All the women inside me / Jana Elhassan; translated by Michelle Hartman.
Other titles: Aná, hiyá wa-al-ukhrayāt. English
Description: Northampton: Interlink Books, 2021.
Identifiers: LCCN 2021001562 | ISBN 9781623718862 (paperback)
Subjects: LCSH: Women—Fiction. | Interpersonal relations—Fiction. |
      Abused women—Fiction. | GSAFD: Psychological fiction
Classification: LCC PJ7930.J36 A5313 2021 | DDC 892.7/37—dc23
LC record available at https://lccn.loc.gov/2021001562

Printed and bound in the United States of America

To Nelson Mandela

"Wandering between two worlds, one dead,
The other powerless to be born,
With nowhere yet to rest my head"

—Nelson Mandela quoting Matthew Arnold

CHAPTER 1

I've always stood at a distance from my life and simply let it happen. I've always played the role of spectator. In one way or another, I've dissociated from reality, as if it didn't concern me, as if the visible Me—who lives her life out in the world—is somehow opposed to that other Me—who sits back and observes events. I've existed in a state of perpetual waiting for the Self, that flees only to later return and recount imaginary events, tales more fantastic than those that grandmothers tell their grandchildren. I stored up my dreams in this joyful Self of mine. But whenever I gazed out at the ivory-colored curtains hanging in our house and the emptiness that filled its rooms, I always felt disappointed.

My mother hid all of the crockery, glassware, and little crystal figurines in the house from me. She was convinced that I was going to secretly spread out a blanket on the floor of my room to make a castle or a palace. She thought that I would take all these things out, organize them, and then scatter them around again—so that I could create a fantasy world where I'd be able to spend hours on end talking, whispering, and fighting with my imaginary friends.

But I wasn't sad to find myself alone, without all those things. I used to gaze through the iron bars covering my bedroom window, to contemplate the road and the passersby. That's when I would begin to weave their stories together, trying to guess what they cared about and believed in. Other people have always been a mystery to me. They're a world yet to be discovered. I wanted to find out what this world consisted of—and not out of prurient curiosity alone. This desire saw the light of day even before I took my first breath. The Me who used to tell myself stories lived in the world with these Others, while the other Me remained locked in a cage watching the world pass by from behind bars.

In my relationship with my Self, I always struggled against two powerful, opposing currents: soft, easy proximity and deathly, distorted distance. Sometimes I was a young girl in a sky-blue dress who could touch the heavens. Other times I was a woman dressed in black from head to toe, following the scent of a sarcophagus, waiting for a period of mourning to end.

My father preferred that I remain isolated, far from the dangers of the outside world. He tried to keep me from living life. My mother did the same to herself. Even though I went to school every day, I never experienced freedom. I didn't really interact with the school environment. I did, however, connect with the land on our sporadic visits to my village in the countryside, a faraway place where it's possible to see the sun. But it was too still and empty for a girl like me who always had to be immersed in doing something.

This Other person was found only inside my Self, but in different forms. In bed when I went to sleep, I could be whoever I wanted. In my mind, I used to create and re-create composite pictures of my doll's house. I would deconstruct life and then remake it into other worlds. To be honest, I've always loved the things that existed only inside my own mind. I felt safe weaving facts into my imagination, because then I could experience their specificities and be done with them whenever I wanted to. Although I couldn't always distinguish when I was actually there and when I wasn't, I knew that it was Me who was in control.

I changed with the passing of time. And then I changed and changed again. Today I can barely remember the faces of the people who passed through my life unless I dive deep back into my game and summon them up to reconnect with them one by one. I don't know if this is necessary, or if it stems from trying to know my Self. But is my memory even credible? How could it be, since I've always improvised my existence out of so many unexpected places in order to stay alert? Could these eagerly awaited musings now be plausible? Even if they were, it wouldn't matter. The only thing that can make a radical difference is what is left unsaid. I will go on speaking, however, for one reason only—the pleasure of speaking, the pleasure of revealing things perhaps, and indeed even the pleasure of lying.

I was born and raised in a relatively large house. It was more than 2,000 square feet, evenly divided into closed-off rooms, all separate from one other. The furniture was questionably clean. In the living room, the armrests were always lying vertically, perched at the edges of the sofa, like eyes watching you or silent idols to be worshipped. Everything was in its place: the rectangular table at the center of the room, the telephone always in its same spot on the left. The sides of the tablecloth were draped evenly over the table with care. All the pots were stacked up inside the kitchen cupboards; my mother never changed the way they were organized. The plastic containers rested on the bottom shelf close to the door, and the glassware and dishes were always arranged on the upper shelf.

The jars in the pantry were lined up by size, from biggest to smallest, while the vegetables were stored in a layered basket. There was always a large bowl of fruit in the middle of the table. In the dining room, a set of bohemian cups was on display in a glass case. My mother only took them out if special guests were visiting—to honor them and show off the perfect luster reflected in their refined, elegant crystal.

The extremely precise organization of the furniture made our house seem empty and predictable, vacant and silent—even tedious. Life happened according to a repetitive system, in which mealtime was never impeded by playtime or our studies. There was even a set time for speaking. Food had a specific scent, which was very different from how it tasted. Salt was used in moderation, weighed precisely on a scale, and there was never a bit more or a bit less. We were allowed one small treat per day, in the afternoon, more specifically at 5 PM.

Even if my father was not as rigid as my mother, he seemed completely cut off from real life, always lost in his expansive library. He lived with his books and papers more than he did with us. He spent many long hours with these books. I understood little else about them other than that they were huge, matching the thick glasses he never removed. He set aside one hour each evening to sit with us in the living room. Other than that, we never saw him. During that hour, I deliberately stuck close to him and laughed a lot, despite my mother's scorn for me acting silly. I was trying to create some sort of space for free expression contrasting with the elegant emptiness surrounding us.

I was always with them, but we were never ever together. In my childhood, I was so immersed in those obscure relationships, which connected me to the world around me, that I no longer knew what reality was. I thought that the world functioned only inside of the framework of the family. This meant I was inadvertently caught up in my parents' lives. I didn't realize that I could react to my existence differently until it was too late. But I also did realize that difference came at a price. It was something that money couldn't buy. You pay a painful tax on solitude, whether this solitude is voluntary or coerced.

Now, as I embark upon the third decade of my life, I no longer remember where I left my Self—the Me wandering around outside, fleeing from what resides deep within her. I'll probably never find it, so I involuntarily surrender to all this emptiness. I can no longer see Sahar, except at night when I lay my head on my pillow. She used to come to me in my imagination, pat my head, stroke my hair tenderly and with pity, drawing endless circles of stories about other people to help me fall asleep. It was only with her that I could get a good night's sleep. My big bed always made enough room for all the people I created in my imagination and whom I loved so much but wasn't able to be with.

CHAPTER 2

Though my family comes from a conservative milieu in North Lebanon, religion never played a central role in our identity or our existence. God was totally absent from our house. We didn't have Qur'anic verses or icons of the Virgin Mary hanging on any of the walls. The only tangible evidence of religion in our home was the Qur'an my father kept next to the Bible on the large bookcase that took up an entire wall of his office. This seemed like a gesture to calm the religious and sectarian tensions of a closed environment like ours. But this was not exactly true. The absence of religious symbols and rituals meant that we were missing out on life in another way. We remained suspended in an ambiguous state of impartiality that transformed our life into a dry, flavorless chalkboard.

The two books had an equal standing in our house, as they were equally irrelevant. They were never discussed, but necessary for my family to continue to confirm a godly presence, factually but never spiritually. Some of my father's friends were Christian, and we used to visit them on Christmas and Easter. This put my father into an unusually good mood and caused my mother to grit her teeth, hardly able to spit out two or three words on those occasions.

Our home's harmonious, pastel decor was also devoid of paintings, flowers, or colors. My mother packed all tangible signs of life away in cardboard boxes wrapped in plastic. She had a frightening ability to empty things of their content. The only outward expression we ever saw of this were her spontaneous conniption fits. This woman normally wrapped in quiet would suddenly become crazed and enraged, a bull let loose in front of a red flag. Her apathy would vanish. When she lost her calm and quiet, she became a fierce woman venting a strange sort of wrath.

My mother was like a woman with constant PMS—nerves on edge, bloated belly about to burst. She was not at all the soft flower blowing in the breeze that she could have been. I grieved for the flower of a mother I never had, always seeing her as ugly as disgusting animal innards.

Emptiness wasn't the annoying thing about our house. What is so annoying is my inability to describe it. It was neither good nor bad. There was nothing wonderful about the aesthetics of the house, but nothing grotesque about it either. Silence pervaded it, and that tense, raging scream ran throughout all of us. The place was like a gun with a silencer; there was always continuous pressure on the trigger. Shots were fired and penetrated deep inside our flesh without making any noise at all.

In any case, I knew I was Muslim because our relatives would visit us during Eid al-Adha and Eid al-Fitr, even though we didn't get clothes on those occasions like other children did. I also knew because the sounds of the dawn prayers, emanating from the minaret of the Mansouri Great Mosque of Tripoli, rang out near my grandfather's house right at the bottom of the fortress on the western side of the city. The Great Mosque, as they call it, occupies a large plot of land in the old city. It's characterized by simple architecture, a lack of decoration, and walls covered by a layer of limestone. The north façade overlooking the courtyard has a sundial to determine the exact time of the adhan.

At our house, during Eid, my mother would serve visitors ma'amoul and ghraybeh cookies, accompanied by cinnamon tea. Despite my father's categorical refusal to accept the traditional Eid gifts of money from anyone, my grandfather would stuff coins in our pockets and give us sweets that we would hurriedly devour before he left, for fear that my mother would take them away.

We interacted with the Eid like spectators who craved it because it surrounded us on all sides. But we were afraid of it too: afraid to come too close or to truly engage. My father's holiday-boycott was simply a way to prove his adherence to dreams of socialism and a bygone communism. It was his expression of a built-up series of disappointments, which he blamed on God—a word he never uttered.

My father spent years struggling for the cause of what he called "liberation and social justice." This meant that he denied us, his own children, the right to celebrate religious holidays. To him, they represented the scourge of religion and sectarianism. When he went to Kuwait in the mid-1990s to work in an important research center, he might have been able to radically change his position. But this experience only served to further fuel his resentment and indignation against Arab regimes.

He only ever mentioned his homeland in relation to death and fear. The occupation hit just as he was rushing to flee his city. He found himself confused by the proliferation of so many different factions and parties. He didn't even know where they all came from. He was only certain of one thing: he was a communist. He strove for the loftiest possible goal—a social utopia in which rich and poor would be equal and a decent life within everyone's reach. This wonderful image would satisfy his deeply held idealistic expectations.

He repeatedly expressed his indignation toward the lack of opportunities for young people and the disintegration of life, which resulted from this legacy. His hatred reinforced his alienation from his surroundings. Just as rebellion for the sake of rebellion becomes a way of life, my father's rejection of religiosity and ritual worship made him embrace a shiny new, progressive, partisan law. He grew attached to the new system, whose reach was global. All of this made him feel that he had broken my grandfather's outdated rules and was superior to the people from the neighborhood. He saw them as stuck in their limited lives, their dreams never exceeding the boundaries of the Great Mansouri Mosque. He believed that he was the defender of his own class, the working class, while also somehow feeling that he was better than them.

He told his old friends that he was equipped with a unique and exceptional defensive instinct, as a man who had wholeheartedly embraced his cause, so much so that he would do anything to arouse and pleasure it. This was his promise to the working class. He wanted to bring them justice so that they would never again suffer. As his daughter, I knew the lightness of his spirit only in passing flashes. This makes it difficult for me now to not confess that he'd changed a lot. He reminded me of a bird, soaring high in the sky, who'd forgot he had wings and plummeted to the ground, disillusioned.

After three years abroad in Kuwait, my father returned from the desert wearing a hat known as a "shabka." Wearing it was like confirming to his peers and the whole neighborhood that the Bedouin keffiyeh and long jilbab did nothing for him. Visitors flocked to visit this man who had just returned from the Gulf, convinced that he would offer them Arabian dates and gift them prayer beads. They were surprised by his shabka hat and the picture of Che Guevara prominently displayed on the wall. My grandfather sarcastically disparaged him with a smile, saying: "Anyone who saw you would have thought you'd been in a European country, not among Arabs." My father ignored his visitors' criticisms. He was so determined to keep the framed picture up that my mother eventually relented despite her continued irritation, as she had not changed her decor or even added one new piece of furniture for years.

My father's shabka hat remained the talk of the neighborhood for several months. One shopkeeper even invented a story for his clients that my father had gone mad in Kuwait after being afflicted by sunstroke and fainting in the desert. The story varied depending on the narrator. Some thought a jinni had possessed my father's body. Others thought that he had taken drugs while he was away. The women of the neighborhood turned to God for help, and my Auntie Marwa suggested that my mother should consult Shaykh Bilal so he could diagnose my father's condition. After several attempts, she eventually managed to convince my mother to visit this man who could undo the effects of magic and the evil eye.

My mother brought me with her on this visit to Shaykh Bilal. I was the buffer that would keep her above any suspicion by our neighbors. She warned me a thousand times not to tell a soul about the visit and I agreed completely. A hidden fire burned inside of me. It tried to break away from the dangers of this new, different, and real world. And I wanted to see this "miracle man" as my auntie used to call him. I'd started believing that he was one of God's helpers and that he would thus be able to offer me a clearer picture of the Creator.

We wove through the narrow, dark alleyways before finding ourselves in front of a big door topped by a large white stone arch made of smaller, alternating black and white stones. We were on the southern edge of the city near the Bab al-Raml cemetery, next to the Arghun Shah Mosque. The shortcut to where we were going led us through the cemetery and we trod upon its overtaxed land, filled with waste, grass, trash, and trees broken by the wind. Sewers, forgotten graves, and roofs of kiosks stood guard silently. My auntie quickened her step; her body wrapped in her black abaya seemed familiar with the dead and the land embracing them. My mother followed closely behind her, trying to keep up with her pace, holding the edge of her simple, loose, white polka-dotted cotton dress with many pockets.

At last we arrived in a neighborhood packed tight with buildings stacked precariously atop each other, their walls leaning against one another for support, a reflection of the spirit of the community residing within them. I saw children playing and having fun in the streets, despite their obvious poverty and the difficulty of their lives there. Lost for a moment thinking how it would be impossible to join in and play with them, I looked up and found myself in a more expansive neighborhood, where buildings were spaced out and their windows closed.

We entered a large, four-bedroom apartment after being greeted by a large woman in her forties, a beauty spot with a hair sprouting out of it just above her upper lip.

Shaykh Bilal was not what I expected. He was huge and

ugly. He had large, prominent, yellowed teeth and harsh features. I sensed no cruelty in him, but I felt afraid, as if the stones of my house were crushing me. He began eying my mother suspiciously and she remained silent, like she didn't know how to tell her story because the words might melt away.

When she tried to speak, her words got tangled up and stuck in her throat. I sat in the corner of the room, contemplating the two of them with fear and awe, like a painting on the wall that witnessed what was going on between the owners of the house and their neighbors. Whenever my eyes met his, I wanted to cry—from the sheer gloomy horror of his appearance, but also from the fear instilled within me of everything and everyone to do with religion.

My auntie took over and started talking about the character of her sister's communist husband, in the language of chaotic, popular local proverbs. Despite her loquacious narrative, she confused past and present tense, pronouns and adjectives. She spoke rudely and harshly. She told the shaykh that my father didn't have sex with my mother and that she was pretty sure he was "not quite right."

The shaykh nodded his head, indicating that he was following along with Auntie Marwa, stealing glances at my mother and stroking his long beard. My auntie kept on talking, saying that my mother tried to touch my father once and he pushed her away and slept on his stomach, breathing deeply and rhythmically like a child who was full after dinner. The shaykh whispered a few words in my mother's ear and called to the woman who had first led us to him. He asked her to bring my mother a stone. He counseled her to put it under my father's bed without him knowing.

In the following weeks, my mother started going into my father's office, checking that the door was locked, and then lighting incense, all the while mumbling strange words that I couldn't hear or understand. I watched her through the peephole. She even wrapped one of his books in a large crimson-and-yellow-striped velvet cloth, then tucked it into my auntie's purse along with I don't know how many banknotes.

My mother didn't know if she was actually religious, or if indeed she should be. She didn't really care about his shabka hat. She also didn't know much about whether or not God existed, but she had memorized some verses of the Qur'an and felt a powerful and real need not to stray too far from the Islamic social norms she had been raised with. Marrying my father tore her away from them. She refused to believe that he had grown so distant from these social norms because of something within himself. She preferred to lay the responsibility for his estrangement on divine powers. Deep down, though, she only really cared about one thing: why her husband didn't treat her better.

My mother was a woman so delicate it was as if she were encased in glass. She wanted my father to desire her and crave her desperately. She wanted him to be in love with her, like a dog drooling over a piece of meat. She wanted to drain his love of the Soviet Union from his veins and transfuse them with love for her. She wanted to joyfully decorate our house with vases, and to add a little flavor to both her cooking and our lives. But her feelings remained forever folded up and put away. She spent many long hours in front of the mirror closely examining how she looked. She sometimes tied her hair up in a bun and measured the size of her ears to make sure they were equal and symmetrical. She drew her eyebrows on with a brown pencil, painted her lips ruby red, and finished it all off with a dab of blush on her cheeks.

When she opened the door to greet my father, however, he'd pass in front of her without saying anything about how she looked. She was simply something he did not see. He hardly ever addressed a word to her. He would just sit down on his usual chair and wait for her to bring him a hot, well-cooked meal, with no scent or spice.

After he ate, he would go into his room, take a bottle of vodka out of his secret cabinet, pour himself a little glass, and drink it slowly. He always had three types: Beluga, Stolichnaya, and Moskovskaya. He took care to drink a different one each night. He would listen to one of his old records and close his eyes, his features shrinking. He would then get into bed and sleep deeply. My mother always felt nauseated washing the last traces of alcohol from his cup while reciting Qur'anic verses and cursing my father's communist and Christian friends.

My auntie brought my mother a bottle of Arabian perfume that Shaykh Bilal had told her to wear. As if prescribing medicine whose dosage must always be exact and never forgotten, she told her to spray it under her arms, on her neck, and between her breasts every morning and evening. My mother carefully obeyed all of the orders of the man who she believed would finally solve all of her problems. She implemented them faithfully and without complaint.

The skaykh's requests began to increase a little at a time. When my auntie began to see my mother's patience waning, she reassured her with each payment to him that it would be her last. She said that Hajj Bilal was blessed—he did not take the money for himself but rather distributed it to the poor and needy, and this would earn my mother the goodwill of God and his messengers. One time my mother told my auntie, tucking a golden chain into her purse, "May God grant a good result."

When she saw no change in her husband's condition, she proclaimed Shaykh Bilal a charlatan and a hypocrite. My auntie's eyes grew round and her face blazed red hot as if she'd been slapped across the face. Even her hair seemed to be burning in anger. She placed her hand over her sister's mouth, saying, "Shut up. You're the one whose husband doesn't even believe in God—not at all. This man is not possessed by the jinn, he's possessed by demons from head to toe. You should look at what you all are doing to God before you start talking about shaykhs."

She tied her scarf back around her head and rushed out of our house, asking God to grant her refuge from her sister's unbeliever of a husband. She slammed the door angrily, leaving my now penniless mother all alone with her bad luck. The silence that dominated the room was filled with the battle between Good and Evil, and empty of everything else. My mind was bursting with the thought of God, who had always been forbidden to us, a stranger whom my auntie claimed we'd offended.

CHAPTER 3

People in the neighborhood stopped criticizing my father with the passage of time. They found him unexpectedly condescending and distant. Even though he often was just bored, he gave the impression that he was extremely distracted and therefore disconnected from the realities surrounding him. For a long time, he managed to simply watch life, locked away in his own private world, as if everything around him was fading away. He liked to believe he was busy with loftier and more important issues than those men who spent their days at the Mousa Cafe, busy with their dice games and the bubbling water at the bottom of their argilehs.

He didn't watch television and considered it an enemy of culture. He left that to my mother, who would stretch out on the sofa and flip through the channels to find an Arabic movie to watch. He did, however, tune into the news every evening at 8. He reacted irrationally to every broadcast, as if he always needed there to be an "event"—and not just any event, but something big and important, unlike the life he was living.

A certain fragility alleviated his alienation in the hours he spent with us. We all felt freer, and he even stopped talking in his grandiose style with its strangely complex pronunciation, which often made him seem rude and dry. At times, I found his funny stories about adventures all over the world amusing.

I often thought that he was actively feuding with God. I wondered how he could be so loving and arrogant at the same time, both liberated and stuck in place. He was taciturn; he corralled his tongue, as if words strangulated him. My mother watched him through the cracks of the huge divide that separated them, her admiring gazes slowly turning into hatred, rage, and jealousy. When we sat together to eat, she chewed slowly, with no appetite, trying hard to swallow her food. She was full after two or three bites.

Once my father asked her to eat more. Her facial features suddenly changed, as if a miracle had taken place right before her eyes. She looked confused and started stuttering. She tried to make her voice sound balanced, refined, and even somewhat theatrical, moving her hands around and ostentatiously dishing out the food. Her effort to eat her vegetables seemed to help her regain some happiness and the will to live, as well as her strength and beauty. All of this happened because of his one simple request and sudden concern about what she was eating.

Now, when I look back at how her face lit up at that one lone dinner, I also remember how she used to convulse and groan during her intermittent insomnia. She suffered from panic attacks, especially with my father's seemingly endless absences and travels abroad. I knew about her disappointment and loneliness from looking through the peephole at night. By day, I sensed it from the harsh standstill at home. She was haunted by constant feelings of distress, anger, and a fierce desire to save face.

She had an image of the ideal close family. What was missing from ours was any kind of communication, and there was almost no physical contact between her and my father.

My mother's body was solid. She stood as straight as a column, artificially trying to deny her lumps and bumps. When she stretched out on the sofa, her round breasts suddenly appeared, popping out like sardines from a tightly packed tin. The curves of her buttocks struggled to emerge as well from her body that was stuffed into the furniture as if between the edges of an abyss. Her hair hung halfway down her back in a beautifully feminine way; any signs of masculinity would detract from her charms. I used to imagine my wooden mother peeling off from her true self in that exact position and exposing how she was actually as soft and gentle as water. One fact I discovered is that my mother was neither as strong and tough, nor as stupid as my father tried to make her out to be. The poor woman was simply trying to use her authority and domination to colonize any and all spaces of freedom—not to enjoy them, but to suck the life out of them.

I discovered another thing growing up—that my father was not as intelligent as he tried to convince everyone he was. My father was only a human being to me during playtime. Aside from this, I saw him in the same way I did all other beings and people: as totally separate from me. I rejected the foolishness and false concern that he cloaked himself in. Like my mother, I kept my image of him distant from me in my mind. I held both their worlds apart from my own and kept myself busy playing alone with my dolls in my imaginary world.

I stared out of my window at the abandoned building in the garden across from our house for hours on end. Yellow paint was peeling off sections of the building, which was crumbling because of the war, or as people around here prefer to say, "the events." I looked out at the empty, exposed rooms and stone-filled rubble, where a ghost regularly appeared, emerging from the crumbling concrete: a gray-haired man who looked a lot like my father but was more agile as he climbed through the debris.

In my mind, I conjured up the people in my neighborhood. I imagined a woman for that old man, and they came together emotionally and intimately. My imagination decorated those empty walls with several paintings, and children having fun in the hallway while the aroma of delicious food cooking emanated from the kitchen. The house filled with visitors, music, Eid gifts, ma'amoul, other cookies, and everything else that I found missing in our empty, harsh, and fake existence. My mother's voice always used to wrench me out of these daydreams, because girls weren't supposed to spend hours sitting and staring out of windows and balconies.

I always obeyed her orders without objecting. I would drag myself to where she wanted me to be and bid the people in my other life farewell in peace, until our next meeting.

As I mentioned before, the nothingness surrounding me has always contradicted my inner world, which nearly consumed me because of how loud and busy it was. In any case, anxiety has been my constant companion since childhood. I used to sometimes feel dizzy with this inner thirst for a life that was richer, less routinized, and more exciting.

My heart yearned to find a normal rhythm inside my chest. At certain moments, I even reckoned it was swollen because of how it expanded, then calmed down again like a stray cat react-ing to another's meow. That emptiness always made me panic. Sometimes I couldn't even distinguish whether this feeling came from inside me or was pouring into me from the outside. On several occasions, I spent time with my mother and siblings only to reassure myself that I was still alive and present.

My siblings and I were often quick to bicker, and my mother would shout, "Be quiet! Do you think you are the only ones in the room? Stop talking like this. All your noise is going to be the end of me!" She would then change how she was sitting, knit her hands together, and stare at us. She suddenly turned into a drill sergeant, surveilling us to keep us from playing. I felt that we were locked into performing a repetitive and inelegant comedy routine that generally did not end well.

CHAPTER 4

When I accompanied my mother to the beauty salon, I spent my time comparing her hair to that of the other women there. She was never the kind of woman to have her hair washed outside of the house. She was someone who always personally checked the ingredients of every product she used. In all her dealings both with us and with other people, her meticulousness was evident. Her lips shaped the words she pronounced with an affected and pretentious elegance; she curved her hand gracefully to tuck a lock of hair back behind her ear.

For some time after we'd returned back home, all of this pretense would disgrace her and expose her coldness. Her dark, depressed eyes expressed her longing to go out in the world. Her delicate nose inhaled the scents of the outside air in vain, and her ears perked up to overhear various things happening in the neighborhood: the merchants calling out from the hardware shops, and the barking of stray dogs that desired a greater destiny than the misery surrounding them.

Sometimes she would ramble on to herself in long monologues lamenting her fate, like a bereaved mother who'd lost her only child: "You see, Suad, it's one step forward and one step back. There's no money and no love. Even your short, stupid sister looks down on you. But what can I do? You have no luck, so don't bother even trying. God grants things only to those who don't actually need them." But then she'd retreat a bit, "*Astaghfirullah*, forgive me, forgive me God."

There were moments when I felt a strong desire to embrace her and bring some color back to her sunken cheeks. I would steal a quick smile from her as she ran her fingers through her hair. I wished we could just sit and talk like mother and daughter, but her pallor always quickly returned. Silent despair tore at my heart. It was more painful than any call of distress, more piercing than the baying of wolves.

When I was growing up, I didn't know how much I resembled my mother or if I would eventually become cold and volatile like her. But, in my adolescence, I noticed that I was training my body to be a featureless soldier lined up for morning roll call. I hated the way I sat. My back hunched over, and my suspicious thighs were clenched together as if purposely strangling my vagina. Terror afflicted me when my breasts swelled and filled out my chest.

I wore long flowing blouses throughout my teen years, embarrassed of showing any signs of femininity. My mother bought them for me in various sizes and colors; I didn't leave this uniform behind until I went to university. I looked odd around the other girls of my age who wore different kinds of clothes. My face, the way I walked, and even the color of my skin resembled these shirts. The features of my body were erased by the way my mother layered these shirts atop each other, so I looked like a mannequin for a garment factory that produced ready-made, look-alike fabrics.

My father was silent about this singular, but color-changing, shirt of mine. He and my mother silently colluded about the need to hide any possible relationship between my body and life out in the world. I wasn't allowed to wear a thin hijab or change my hairstyle. This is how my father ensured that I would remain isolated from femininity. I knew that the two of them feared and hated any sense of femininity. My auntie finally broke this fashion cycle. She convinced my mother that I should be able to look elegant, because if I carried on looking like a boy, no one would ever want to marry me.

Nothing struck more fear in my mother's heart than the idea that I was reaching marriageable age. She feared that I might be a spinster, because the extended family believed that she hadn't done a good job bringing me up. She was less disturbed by the idea of me being without a man than her own failure to present the model of a happy family—like the one in the photo album that she kept locked away in the bottom drawer of her wardrobe, far from us children.

Whenever one of her relatives or girlfriends visited us, she deliberately brought her precious treasure out of quarantine and displayed it to those present. "This is a picture of Sahar at the school party. This is me, pregnant with her brother. This is a photograph of me on my engagement day." She would then close her eyes and tell her usual tale of how she met my father on a visit to his sister who was one of her girlfriends. She admired him as he thumbed through a foreign newspaper, and deliberately attracted his attention by pretending to be interested in international affairs and news about the insurgents. Whenever she told the story, she stopped for a brief moment, and a low humming rose from deep within her. Her limbs shrank, and she released a long sigh that hearkened back to an earlier time, when she didn't know that her life with this man would lead to chronic insomnia, and the tightness in her throat spread sadness within her from head to toe.

CHAPTER 5

I don't remember specifically when the first man entered my bed, but I am certain that it happened when my father was abroad in Kuwait. Despite my efforts to get rid of him, I couldn't escape him for one whole, long night. Several men filled the room and the courtyard facing the spacious garden. This provided the thrill and excitement that I needed in an environment filled with fine china. He looked at me through the crowd. He approached and retreated. As soon as I looked back, he all but disappeared.

For a split second he wasn't there anymore. My eyes darted around, searching for him, and I felt a hand on my shoulder. He was there. His face was dark, his features strange and somewhat sad. I slid over and made a place for him to lie down next to me. I rested my hand against his forehead. I touched his eyes, lips, neck, and leaned my head upon his chest, desperate for him not to resist when I reached out for him. A moment later, however, he no longer existed. I cried myself into a deep sleep.

This was the first time that I admitted to myself that I needed strong and loving feelings. I realized how much I missed my father, and how lonely I was. I preferred to speak to this imaginary stranger and throw myself into his arms than to be alone. He came to me in bed every night. I got naked in front of him and he touched my body. I gave him a name and let him take me to a different place every night, according to his desires. When I awoke every morning, I found nothing but traces of his shadow. I always forgot how things ended between us. I left things open.

In real life, however, I was extremely unhappy. All this time, I was determined to relieve my body of the intense work of living in the world. I knew by heart the fairy tales about princesses who were rescued by knights from the jaws of the dragon. I also knew of the words mumbled by charlatans—most of whom were somehow connected to my auntie and Shaykh Bilal. I had to save myself from their clutches. I had to become the kind of girl who could wander freely and unconstrained right into the heart of the forest. The chasm between me and my life widened; I found my Self getting lost and hiding from Me. My life inclined toward somewhere else, frantic voices imploring it to come closer. It steps forward, like a little girl before she's become a woman. I entered basements and dark corridor-like tunnels, several times. A sense of despair lasting for several days would at times overtake me and I would lose it. This made me slip into protracted periods of loneliness, as if I'd lost something not imaginary but very real.

My habit of conjuring up a man in my head until I fell asleep became a habit. Despite the constraints of my actual existence, these fantasies enabled me to plunge into places denied to me. Not only did I have sensory experiences, I also had emotional and intellectual ones. I was in dire need of the Other, even if only a ghost or a fantasy that I'd created to alleviate my loneliness.

In the beginning of my relationship with my fantasies, I waited for this Other person to tell me what to do. I was always under the orders of a supreme authority that guided me and made me feel his power and brutality. This developed as I matured. My sexual fantasies were no longer based on submissiveness or waiting for a man to take the initiative out of my own fear of doing it. I became more active. I tried to take charge of things, making love until I reached orgasm and not stopping until my body had achieved maximum pleasure.

Most of the time my imagination was very refined. I had idealistic dreams about love and giving. I created the romance we were denied at home in my own mind. I fell in love with totally imaginary men. My body moved in my bed, with shallow and evenly spaced breathing, and I saw them moving inside me. This Other person could have been real, but it was impossible for me to find him. He was like a cloud of smoke become incarnate before me, clothed in the space of the room. I would chase him until he evaporated. Now looking back, I ask myself, how many men did I know in my imagination… ten, or more? I don't even know.

Were all those fantasies actually helpful? Perhaps they were simply a rejection of the coldness we were living through at home. I know that I was fleeing to imaginary men so I could cling onto their bodies and satiate my thirst for recognition by someone called "Me." I was refusing to end up like my mother. Sin races through my mind so I can find some salvation in it. There was a little girl hiding inside of me, a girl forbidden to play, surrounded by harshness; I was trying to regain her stolen rights. Perhaps my choice to study interior design was definitive proof of my disgust at our empty house. This choice, of course, alarmed my mother. She believed I should study something more serious that had nothing to do with art.

Art is an expression of creativity. To my mother, creativity was something subversive, outside of the norm. It was not something one should acquire, because it would always make a mess of things. Creativity compromises how life should be, our customs, traditions, and habits. This is why she was so keen that the furniture of our house never be changeable or replaceable. It had to be appropriate, neat, and not necessarily lively. Whenever I brought her furniture catalogs and tried to explain how over-lapping fabrics could create a look different from what we were used to, her indifferent reaction was meant to let me know that her convictions about this were firm. There was no way even one piece of furniture in the house would be changed. She couldn't stand being surrounded by beautiful things: it would trigger all of the sadness she had stored up in her heart and that had eventually become her only way of life.

Everyone around me was so wrapped up in their own social lives they couldn't live. Meanwhile, this imaginary Other Person inside me could live freely, though it was difficult for me to reach out to him and laugh. I used to need him so badly. I also feared him to the point that I was in denial he existed. Even if I tried to separate from him, he dwelt within me. When I say it like that, it sounds crazy. But was I ever anything else? Wasn't I just yearning to be filled like the emptiness I was surrounded by? Didn't those thoughts run through my mind until I was spent by the idea of my presence and his absence?

All of this was my attempt to crush tedium and live my life. Looking back at the few times my mother deigned to pay me the slightest bit of attention and talk to me about life is still incredibly painful to me. There were so many times I intended to tell her about what was worrying me. I even geared myself up to talk to my father. But the words would simply fall back inside me and remain lodged there. This Self of mine remained a painful connection to them. It besieged me but led me nowhere. Today I am haunted by questions. They are still stuck in my throat, forever on the verge of being uttered. They remain swallowed, replaced by a meek, submissive smile. As if I were invisible.

I was jealous of my siblings' ability to engage with reality, while I remained outside of it. They whispered to each other, sitting on the straw chairs lined up in our kitchen. They did silly things that would arouse the ire of my mother. They immediately grew silent if she shouted at them, but always went back to whatever they were doing the second she was out of earshot. Every time I tried to join in and imitate them, I felt small, sad, fragile, and weak. I couldn't keep up with their silliness or simplicity.

I also couldn't convince myself that we really were a happy family. I realized deep down that happiness would never be a part of our household. When I started studying interior design, I spent many hours planning different decors for our house. I imagined it filled with colors. I designed a wood-burning stove and searched for a suitable place to put it. The fireplace was not only intended to keep the family warm and protected from the harsh winter. It also symbolized something much more important—family warmth. Wrapping up and gathering together in front of it on bitter cold winter evenings would help to create an intimate atmosphere, countering the coldness of our vacant, familial relationships.

But none of this worked. We always remained precariously on the border between life and nothingness. I realized that something was needed to save me from my bitterness and make me feel that I belonged to my Self or even to someone else. I needed to know that I was not an illusion—that I existed somewhere other than in the realm of ideas. This is what prompted me to cling onto Sami at the beginning of our relationship. His excessive attention to every detail of my existence was beyond compare.

Every morning before he went out on a walk, he would pass by to see me. He would look at me and smile, examining every bit of me, from head to toe, especially my silky brown skin. He smiled with satisfaction whenever my face flushed red, my eyes darted around, my head tipped forward inadvertently, and I rushed headlong into the lecture hall. My childlike behavior didn't bother him at all, indeed he reveled in my innocence and purity. The way I stuttered shyly when talking to him reassured him, because it was a guarantee that I'd never spoken to any man before him. It meant that he would be able to possess my fragile being that might dissipate if someone so much as blew on it, because it wasn't solid or coherent. Perhaps this was because I didn't even know if it really existed.

Sami's interest in me, and his insistence on seeing me every day, was the ultimate recognition that I was visible. This was especially true because he seemed like a nice guy who wanted to be with me more than anything else. I tried to overcome my shyness and seem self-assured and confident with him. But he knew I was acting. He sent strong signals that he liked my shyness and that there was no need to give it up. Whenever I was with him, I felt myself getting smaller. Confronted with his large frame, I felt my already petite stature gradually fading and turning into nothing. I tried to find my Self in him. Therefore, for me, everything that he might say was sacred or an unquestionable, absolute truth. Yet I only knew what he told me. I always just faded into the background, on the margins of life.

I didn't truly coexist with reality; it was something that enveloped me. Indeed, I circled around it from a position of extreme longing and a desire to hear my own breathing, to smell my own scent, to touch my own hair, to be sure that I was there—somewhere. To be. With Sami, I existed, and I was prepared to listen. At least I took on some sort of shape when I was with him, even if it was the one that suited him. He used to tell me what he liked me to wear; he bought me a lot of jewelry, especially oddly shaped bracelets. He never complained about me tying my curly hair back. When we were alone, however, he often asked me to untie my ponytail, so he could run his fingers through my hair. This gave me a sudden shiver that ran throughout my entire body. Because I was a person of few words, he always took over. He seemed to enjoy controlling the course of events, immersing us in lessons on how a good girl should behave in today's world.

"Will you continue drawing after we get married?"

"Probably, it is something I've always done."

"How much time do you spend drawing?"

"There's no fixed amount of time."

"Why do you draw?"

"To create beauty."

"Do you know what might be nicer?"

"No."

"An interest in the family."

"But they are two very different things, no?"

"Yes, but you might not have time to draw."

"What would keep me so busy?"

"Me. Don't you want to be with me?"

"Yes, I do want that."

I knew that he was very jealous right from the start. He hovered around me and monitored everything I did. Sometimes it felt as if I were living in a constant state of scrutiny, so I elected not to tell him about all the images burning in my mind. I even began to rein in my thoughts, saving them for when I was asleep. When he entered my imaginary world, I always created the most expensively designed house possible for us, with curtains stretched out along an entire wall, plush chairs, and little tables with ceramic figurines on them. Giant furniture embodied the new life I planned and the aura I created around Sami, my future husband.

He was the savior who would rescue me from my parents' misery. He would allow me to find some kind of independence. He would drown me in bracelets and colors. For a girl like me who dared not even lift her gaze to confront her relatives, or raise any objection to her Self being suppressed, it took the utmost courage to disobey my family and the strict directive never to talk to a man I did not already know. My resentment turned into secret disobedience. Because I was resisting what they expected of me, I reckoned that the contradiction between not being with Sami and suddenly being surrounded by him made the latter the right thing to do. I decided that my path to salvation would come from doing the opposite of what was expected of me.

Sami was raised religious. But he didn't regularly observe the daily rituals of religious practice like praying and fasting. He justified this as due to a lack of time or being ill. He was very keen on his Islamic identity, however. It gave him a feeling of superiority over other religious groups and sects. My future husband believed that Christians couldn't go to heaven, that it was reserved for a specific group of Muslim elites. For him, and all his family, faith was as intransigent and condescending, as it was utilitarian. They mixed religion and God with class stratification.

Sami talked about God the Creator as a way to make blatant reprimands. He used his religiosity in a battle against everything that didn't fit in with his views. As for me, I was eager to enter this religious environment in any way I could. I started drawing mental images of this god—the ultimate power that Sami used to talk about. I thought of him as a sort of sales agent for a furniture company. It was as if the better I acted, the better chance I had of getting another piece of good furniture. I would smile coyly, waiting for my divine reward.

Whenever I went back home, I would gaze on my father with pity. He'd become no more than a failed textile producer, who made things for the home like ready-made curtains and drapes, though I knew he'd never cared about the trade at all. I insisted on labeling him a lower-ranking merchant. I viewed my obstinate father, who refused to hang Ayat al-Kursi on the living room wall, as practically a demon on the way to the underworld where unbelievers burned.

Nevertheless, my interest in religion remained superficial. It revolved around myself and finding the other side of my family—my grandfather, my auntie, and others. All of these people had constantly reminded us to comply with rites and rituals—everything from head covering to going to the mosque on Fridays. God was a societal modality that allowed them to engage the people of the neighborhood. Religion made them more accepted and even loved by everyone. This was the opposite for us, especially my father, who was ostracized for being different, atheist, Other. He had no place among them.

He was also a mysterious man who everyone wanted to get close to. People were intrigued by the image of the intellectual who liked to sit by himself in cafes for hours at a time. Though he was ostensibly uninterested in others, he was actually there to engage in conversation and debate as he drank hot tea and browsed through newspapers and magazines. It was expected that he would treat the servers badly and arrogantly demand things, while still remaining gracious. The tea was always either too cold or too hot, and the coffee was never boiled long enough. These criticisms were simply a way to show people around him that he knew more than everybody else. He sipped a bit of his drink, smoked a cigarette or two, and raised his eyebrows while reading the newspaper as if he had just discovered a secret of why the Arab world was in crisis or how to develop and grow Third World economies.

My mother saw him just as the rest of the neighborhood did, as a rich master to be served with humility, appreciation, fear, devotion, and limitless tolerance. This was simply because he always seemed to be engaged in something deep that was far beyond their capacity to absorb.

But this wasn't actually true. What are the achievements of a delusional master who'd spent more than a decade weeping over an idealized past? It seemed to me that in my father's reckoning, time stopped at a single moment—the collapse of the Soviet Union, more specifically the fall of the Berlin Wall and the end of socialist East Germany. He'd spent a few years there and thought it was invincible.

The collapse of the Berlin Wall seems to have, even now, continued to reverberate in my father's ears, as if everything that came afterward was no more than an illusion, turning surrounding events into a mirage. Workers remained oppressed and patronage networks remained in control. His friends died, and he didn't marry a revolutionary woman as he had wished to. No one recognized his brilliance. The Berlin Wall collapsed, bowing down to unbridled capital that preyed on human lives. With his magnificent dream gone, my father withdrew from life. He was too prideful and unable to enjoy anything—fatherhood, work, or even sleeping with his wife. His penis was a forgotten appendage that had forgotten how to get erect and refused to enter any woman apart from his widow, the revolution.

CHAPTER 6

Sometimes facts threaten the truth. We carry on with our pre-planned life how we think it is supposed to be, and the universe influences us in ways we don't even realize. I lost the pleasure of delving into my own exciting, deep, luminous, and impossible imagination for several years. I felt as if an entire life had passed without me knowing if I was truly alive. Many times, I experienced a real desire to be absent, disappear, and become that lack which was the only thing I had ever known since my childhood.

As I mentioned at the outset, throughout my childhood I was governed by desire. That desire developed and took on different forms at every stage of my life. My relationships with men, all of which existed exclusively in my imagination and fantasies from early adolescence, were limited to flirtation. This all changed after I got married. It was as if my libido was expanding and being lured into my very being. My Self needed it to be sure of its existence. I had to free my Self of everything in order to reach deep inside. To be credible, this couldn't be external, but rather had to come from within me.

I used to love men. I longed for a masculine presence in my

life. I imagined myself in my lover's arms, hypnotically sleepy. My face would be lit up by the beam of the streetlight filtering through the window, my features in a state of complete surrender. My loveliest inspirations came when I was completely calm and quiet, at the peak of tranquility. This happened when I was able to be at home alone. That's when I would reach deep in my imagination to become very fragile, trembling like a tiny bird that would die if handled too roughly. This was who I was, a little girl equipped with an exceptionally well-developed survival instinct, who desired flirtation and pampering but was afraid to laugh too loudly for fear that someone might try to take her away.

Perhaps marriage was a way for me to legitimize this desire and give it an acceptable cover. I found myself panicked whenever Sami left me for one reason or another, so I was determined to offer him total obedience to ensure he would remain near me. When he officially asked for my hand, I was confused and even a bit lost, but eager. Sami and his parents came to visit my family. I was terrified of how my father would behave, and my mother was deeply concerned that he might embarrass us in front of the guests by sharing what he thought were wonderful insights and opinions. My father didn't welcome guests like most fathers normally do. Were it not for the presence of my aunt and her husband, my fiancé would have run away and never come back. After everyone had left, my father sequestered the two of us in his room. Shoulders slumped and head bowed, he seemed to be floating in the yellow light emanating from his table lamp. He asked me, "Do you want to get married, sweetheart?"

Embarrassed, I nodded my head. He looked at me again and said, "Aren't you young yet to marry?" I didn't know what to say. It was one of those moments that felt like a gap in time had opened up, forcing us to realize that we never talk. The way my father was looking at me revealed how much distance had come between us over the years. We were quiet until my father broke the silence with a long sigh, "OK, darling, everything will be all right."

I married Sami. This fulfilled my mother's desire to have successfully produced a happy family in the traditional sense. I experienced marriage only as becoming something else and escaping a pallid, suffocating life. I had lost my ability to tolerate that life over time: I spat on myself and raged against it to crush the germs that infected me.

At my simple wedding celebration, all the women I'd invited were old—my mother's and auntie's friends. They wore tight corsets and nylon stockings, refined with their blown-out hairstyles or head coverings, and all wore lots of jewelry: rings, bracelets, and necklaces. I watched my dad puffing on his Cohiba cigar, another attempt on his part to appear naturally refined and polished. Meanwhile, my mother was busy showing off as if our home were the pinnacle of organization and cleanliness. I was shocked to see my grandparents smiling, glowing in a way I had never seen them do previously. That's when I realized that the moment of celebration for girls is not when they are born but when they find a husband. I thought about all those young women who were called old maids, who live their entire lives without seeing that smile of satisfaction traced on the faces of their family members. I now felt I was better than these women, simply because I had found a husband. I was bidding farewell to the Self my parents had given birth to. I felt proud and triumphant because I'd found another entity that I could be. I would rid myself of my non-existence.

I asked Sami to buy lots of paintings to hang on the walls of our house, in retaliation against the emptiness of my childhood home. Knowing how terrible all of those years of boredom and wasted space were, I was determined to find a new existence in my marriage, a paradise, some kind of reality from the imagination that controlled me.

This is how I came close to existing. I was determined to chuck my entire past into the garbage. Arm in arm with Sami, I was full of hope that I might finally discover how to be a woman. I started thinking about how life mocks us, in ways we don't realize, but also compensates us for what's happened before. Sami was the new Other, the opposite-Other, different from the relentless absurdity that was all I had ever known.

Our marriage meant I would stop being merely any girl among the people. I was now someone's wife. A man had recognized my importance. He enjoyed watching me and owning me. I enjoyed throwing my nihilism at him so he could grab hold of it. I felt comfortable giving him my Self, which was always in flight, so he could hang onto it. Or I would become a part of him. This meant my existence no longer concerned only me, but that Other person had now become a destination for me. I had freed myself of the burdens of daily life and achieved a certain degree of security because I no longer existed only inside of my Self.

I felt grateful to him, and so I always did my best to be as dignified, grand, and well mannered as he liked me to be. I thanked him constantly for helping me leave the freezer I had previously been living in. Today I realize that I completely transformed into everything that I had been trying to escape from. I developed a furious desire to laugh, or perhaps to cry, because I waged all my battles with empty hands. I was constantly crushed by feelings stronger than myself, and this had addicted me to deprivation. This was not deprivation in the sense of the denial of joy or pleasure, but the impossibility of convincing myself that I deserved them. I used to ironically touch my face to be sure that I wasn't a mirage. Inwardly, I wanted to disappear and become that nothingness, or laugh for a long time, because I knew that I was merely an accident that life was unprepared for. Even if life were to accept me, I would always feel that I was a burden with no place to be.

My desire often made me cry. I discovered over time that this was not sexual desire, but rather a desire to exist and to prove my being. My body groaned and throbbed like something from primitive times, like a plant pushing up through the soil. I closed my eyes and electricity surged through my body, revealing things that were higher than my own level of understanding and consciousness to my passionate, eager Self.

In my fantasies, which I turned round and round in my head, I felt the Other person's tongue moistening my breasts. He cupped them in the palm of his hand, as if holding a precious diamond, drawing circles around them and making me quiver. I would lean my head back, closing my eyes to see what was beyond reality. The hand of the Other person rested on my neck, while he stretched out on top of me—all warm—and received my delicate skin and abandoned body. The scent of his cool, moist breath touched my lips, half-open and fully prepared for pleasure.

This Other would suddenly become real because of the intensity of my attachment to him. I would grab him for a split second, very gently, bury my head in his chest, sinking into silence. I would escape the swamps of gloom, free myself from chaos, and self-pleasure with my imaginary partners until

I could no longer feel my little wet clitoris. It would throb until I finished, feeling that powerful jerk of my legs and the bottom of my belly. I felt relaxed afterwards. I was a ripple in the sea, floating in the calm after a powerful storm. Sometimes I might smile and laugh coyly because I'd stolen a moment of peace and joy from life. I could reach a kind of climax, even though I was someone who had only experienced life's gutters through observing my mother's futile and truncated existence.

CHAPTER 7

Was I always this lonely or did I simply never learn how to be alive? Why did I have to experience the cruelty of sexual arousal in this way? I felt as if I would never be satisfied, but at the same time was haunted by the opposite feeling—that I didn't desire anything at all. Sex for me was an underworld that would lead me to hell and strip me of the idealism I'd inherited from my mother. I sometimes felt the desire to rise above materialism, inferiority, and implicitly sexual intercourse to secure my feminine social status in this way.

Such base instincts are what made me lie down flat on the ground at times. They compelled me to strip off my clothes and rest my bare belly on the tiled floor. I took pleasure in their coldness, which extinguished my inner rage. It would get wet and feel like fragmented bits of rock. Whenever I embraced my lust, I had to scream at the top of my lungs to control it, to prove that I was too powerful to be a decadent woman who worshiped pleasure. I had to prove that I could be Sami's imaginary wife and be like my mother's friends.

Several times after I'd snuck into the bathroom, I turned into a wild animal. I banged my shoulder against the door and bashed my body against the wall. I kept spinning around myself until I calmed down and felt a pernicious numbness in my upper thigh.

I was frequently alone with my stress and anxiety. My mind shattered into pieces that wouldn't stop thinking. When Sami and the children weren't home, my sexual frustration lasted longer than it should have and simply wouldn't settle. I had an overwhelming desire to break down the door I had been contemplating for hours. Its threshold seemed empty, waiting to be crossed so I could go somewhere else. My sadness always ended in a violent revulsion for wood and walls. I longed to see the outside world, but these barriers prevented me.

But what I did and didn't want will never erase the many years of silent anguish and the fear of expressing what was inside of me. My tongue was a ball of flesh hanging from my throat, then rolling itself out only to hide inside whenever I swallowed my voice. My libido was like a fish imprisoned in a small aquarium, swimming around for hours and then dying of boredom, a mere accessory to human life. I used to see myself in the eyes of amphibians who look out at an alien world from their glass cages. They yearn for something they know is there, even if they don't know exactly what it is.

This was my state of mind when my mother walked through the densely crowded local markets with us in tow. I saw bodies of different shapes and sizes in the crowd. Vendors called out the names of their goods, making pretend offers to passersby to entice them into buying. It was full of bright colors and children unlike me, who didn't wear clean clothes and could run freely between the legs of the people walking by. Also, there was the tantalizing scent of ka'ak coming from a little stall. My father had forbidden us from eating anything exposed to the air that was not protected behind glass.

I never knew why she took us to the local markets. She believed that our material circumstances placed us several degrees higher than other beings and that we belonged to the more refined middle-class elite. The feeling that placed the heaviest burden on her was that she was the wife of an intellectual. This meant that she could no longer act spontaneously with friends she once was like—one of the common people.

She carried the disgrace of her bad luck with her—her husband who only touched her on special occasions—that is, to create us, their four children. She cut herself off from her friends. She couldn't risk exposing the fact that he had long ago abandoned her body, her breasts and vagina, now always cloaked in loose underpants two sizes too big so they wouldn't rub against it. She could hardly remember what it felt like for a man to touch her body.

Perhaps this is what motivated her to raid those sidewalks so quickly and voraciously. She was afraid that someone would catch a glimpse of her and that my father would then know that she liked to shop in poor, common areas. He might realize that she wanted to hang up a gold-threaded embroidery of Ayat al-Kursi in the living room. It pained him to discover that she still believed in God, and that she sometimes liked to pray so she could become like her sister, whose husband made love to her daily after the dawn prayers.

My auntie used to describe to my mother how her husband had sex with her in great detail. She talked about the size of his penis, how he slapped her bum as he got ready to ejaculate, and how he would give her several orgasms in a row. I used to feel that my auntie bit her lips just as she reached the part of the conversation where she was having an orgasm, simply to irritate my mother. She enjoyed proving to her that the bourgeois bastard she was stuck with was only good for reading and writing. For her, culture was merely an impediment behind which we hide our misery.

It wasn't particularly important to me what pushed my mother to secretly frequent the local markets. What I do know is that I enjoyed having direct contact with the bodies I saw walking around me there. I liked the loud noise, the real sounds, the mixed nuts in plastic bags. Even the garbage thrown on the sides of the roads was like a living thing.

The sight of cheap pajamas hanging randomly on a street corner, fabrics displayed in storefronts, people busily involved in everyday situations—all of this made me so happy. Still, I remained stuck in life's back seat. Even if I was watching everything from up close, I was forbidden to talk to these beings, to see their mouths moving from close up, to eat an unwashed piece of fruit from a vegetable cart, to unleash my captive Self, to dive straight into this thing called life.

I remained a mirror for everything happening, an animal imprisoned in a circus cage passing through the forest, contemplating its real mother's nature from a distance, unable to rest in her arms. With the passing of time, a man became an urgent, unattainable need. It was like cutting off a breast to feed a baby, without understanding that it also needs arms around it to hold it when it's hungry.

I too needed another body to satisfy my voraciousness, to feel happy, and to be able to laugh. I needed desperately to hear a voice, to wipe away all the dust from the forgotten, obsolete local markets and turn them into joy. I wanted to eat tasty, unhealthy food. I wanted to erase all of those wasted areas of my life and color them with every emotion: anger, sadness, happiness, unhappiness, jealousy, anticipation, disappointment, hope, peace, anxiety. Anything would do—as long as it expressed a feeling other than nothingness.

Though the neighborhoods that we passed through at full speed were haunted by poverty, I felt an intimacy with them. Familiarity had created a certain kind of empathy between the vendors and their customers; there was an art of life and communication in that world whose doors I wished I could break down. Only then could I get beyond my mother's closed off, ironclad features and know what was going on inside of her.

I observed the city in those few hours with mixed feelings. On the one hand, I felt warmth and sympathy toward everyone I saw; on the other, I felt anger and disgust. The streets were bleak and sad, like the sad attempts at yellow smiley faces scrawled on the sidewalks. For a moment, everything around me became shackles. I could hear howling people in desperate need of attention and care. People lived here, the poor to be specific. They lived on less than the minimum, on dreams that cracks in reality can't touch, on imaginations that can't dream, on desires that don't know they're desires, and on a voluntarily weakened consciousness. They lived on a simplicity that's either a sign of fear or a desire for a sense of security, which they know all the better because of the lack of it.

CHAPTER 8

Whenever I try to recall any tangible memory of my relationship with my husband, it leads me to a locked room, closed off and difficult to penetrate. For some reason, his appearance in my life always confused me. He connected me to a visible sense of existing, close to reality and being alive, but at the same time kept me totally distant from my invisible realities, leaving me completely alone. He was the Other. He embodied sexual fulfillment, and how I saw it, but he never took me where I was trying to go. He lay atop me in bed and kissed me voraciously. I am guessing he was trying to ravage as much of my body as possible. He used to enter me quickly, before I even realized what was happening. I often would cry when he was on top of me. I wished he would slow down a little and get me in the mood by showing me some tenderness. But he was always swept away by showing how he could possess me. He wasn't able to make love with me slowly. It was as if the temporal distance between us would reveal how far apart we were and thus our reality: our closeness was not genuine at all.

Within a few moments, I would transform into a little kitten sitting on a narrow road waiting for a big truck to run over it. I could even hear the roar of the engine as I surrendered to my death under his domination. This was how my relationship with him took shape. It was an enormous disappointment compared to my fantasies, which were saturated with images that now seem marvelous. I buried all of my feelings of anger alongside my childhood sorrows. I convinced myself that real life was completely different from dreams. We must surrender to reality without trying to change it. Little by little I became my mother—the woman I had once refused to be.

Sometimes I looked in the mirror and felt that I'd become really ugly. It wasn't that I was featureless, like that state of nothingness that I existed in for many years. But rather I'd started becoming faded and worn down. I'd ballooned out so much I thought I might explode. I was an ugly blob, sinking into a wave of degradation. I wanted to escape or extinguish my Self in some way, so that I could fit in better with how things in life are supposed to be. Today, I no longer know if I'm looking back at my Self or an Other, or why my features change according to the circumstances and the faces I encounter. It's as if women need a man's recognition in order for their beauty to be complete.

I knew that Sami was pursuing me. I wanted to conceal what might frighten him about me—that I masturbated, for example—in various ways. So, I stopped being that blank slate for him to fill in and started filling it in myself. I now know that I was holding on to him, and I acted like someone who was seeking the recognition that she didn't get from her parents. This recognition was much more important than its aftermath and canceled out that Self whose depths I'd not yet explored.

I was prepared to put up with anything for the sake of that piece of paper, that marriage contract. I wanted the feeling of being shackled, but on the safe side of existence. I fell apart in front of him and gave him absolute authority over me. And that is what he needed to assure himself that he truly possessed me. He took away the parts of me that were my own so he could knead and shape me into the model of woman he hungered for.

If my husband appeared calm when he was in control, he grew anxious whenever he sensed a threat or danger. This would happen if I was away from him for even a moment, or when he wasn't my top priority and the sole focus of my attention. He was troubled by the notion that I might not pass every single thing I did by him first. He didn't like that I might possess any knowledge that could undermine his role as my ultimate master or allow me to find a flaw in something he'd said.

I stuck even closer to Sami when my mother was around. I will never forget the day she visited us and took umbrage at the fact that there was a painting on our dining room wall. It suddenly seemed as if she might revolt, and she started insulting the painting. She hated it because it was beautifying reality. When I told her that this painting made life feel like a Swiss chocolate bar, she replied angrily that drawings delude us into believing that there's no such thing as disaster, devastation, or misfortune. Her rush of words made her seem more miserable than you could even imagine. I understood how badly my mother had been injured by time on that day, and I burst into tears.

My husband seized an opportunity after she left. He loved to see me suffer because of my parents. He swore and badmouthed them. I was unable to confront him or answer back because in those moments I was always an orphan deprived of her parents. He would observe the way I acted, smugly, and initiate sex with me, as if I were just a body that had no refuge other than him.

I would acquiesce. There was no feeling of pleasure; I was just that body, that nothingness. He transformed my body into an image, or just a frame, by connecting to it.

Later, he deliberately brought up my father's lack of religion. He told me about the men in his family who copied out Qur'anic verses until their fingers were swollen, how they'd built one of the oldest mosques in the city with their own bare hands. Sami had in his possession a faded, ancient photograph of his family's elders. Most of them were middle-class men, with shaved heads and swollen cheeks, sporting red tarbooshes with black tassels. They wore thick, loose, black sherwal trousers that encircled their large, round bellies. Sami took every opportunity to ridicule my father, who was a bit short statured, had thick eyebrows and hairy nostrils as dark as caves—one of which he kept raised in a state of perpetual doubt or sarcastic mockery. Reluctantly, I stayed silent. If I started showing resentment, I knew I would have to enter into the tense conversation that he was trying to provoke.

At times, I had a desire to insult him or to ridicule his family in return, but I remained quiet and left my other Self the task of slandering him silently out of his earshot. Sami slowly transformed from that Absolute whom I'd fallen for, into a man I abhorred. I hoped to be liberated from the being I was, that he'd cultivated, or the being he was, which I'd become.

When I lost his being within me, my own Self surfaced from an unknown place. I became more intimate with this Self, searching for more details about existence itself. Sami's other side had been laid bare before me, so that I could finally see clearly what I'd not been able to comprehend while searching for shelter. I married him, only half-aware, a woman with no Self.

I left him flowing through me. I endured his madness and fits of anger without understanding them.

I used to stand on the balcony for long periods and watch the laborers working fervently, as if dancing on gravel. I could see them in constant motion, half naked and with tousled hair. I envied them, because they didn't have time to get lost in their thoughts like I did.

Life outside in the sun was natural to them. But there I was inside, watching, dreaming, imagining. I would await Sami's return home with anticipation, feeling afraid when I heard his shoes tapping against the floors of the house. I would immediately leave the balcony and run inside to pretend that I was busy with household chores.

When he was at home for a long time, I would deliberately move slowly down the steps to throw the rubbish into the garbage can. Before going back up the stairs, I would briefly lean against the wall and contemplate our Russian neighbor, who swept her balcony day and night. I asked myself why she'd gotten married, since she came from a country with freedom and loose women, according to my mother. In fact, I ruminated on all of our female neighbors—venerable women and their modern daughters. Watching them made me ponder why we women are raised to think we have no right to participate in public life, and why they keep us away from the world, especially after we have children.

From the moment I found out I was pregnant for the first time, I was forced to think about having sons: this is what was expected of me and I never dared contradict this expectation. I became another version of my mother—and a harsher one. If my father's indifference diminished his wife, Sami's possessiveness, the imposition of his control over me, and his constant abused and beatings turned me into a little hatchling, feeding off the Other to grow.

My mother destroyed her own desires. She wrapped them up and buried them deep underground like a mummy. I, on the other hand, was governed by my inner desires, before I even realized they were desires. I instead decimated my Self, by transforming into an instrument of pleasure for Sami. The only thing he led me to was the scent of death. How else could it be? He had reduced me to a body of ashes that he quickly devoured and groomed for abuse.

I've always asked myself if it is the fate of all women to cry into their pillows at night, after their husbands fall sleep, because they are confused as to whether or not they themselves exist. Is the destiny of women linked only to their husbands' character? Today I compare my own tears to those of my mother, and I cannot believe that my world has become so bleak.

CHAPTER 9

No doubt, I met the man who would become my husband late. I was very cautious at the beginning of our relationship because I thought if he suspected all of my obsessions and the imperfections in my personality, he wouldn't have married me. I waited with calm anticipation. I never observed him up close before I got together with him. He took me away from the nothingness I was immersed in. During the nights we spent together, I fell asleep in the hope that our commitment to each other would allow me to achieve many things—especially my freedom and existence.

My husband's true colors began to show in his absolute rejection of my father's communism, and persistently reminding me that my unreligious upbringing made my father a piece of trash. He spoke about my father as if he were a kind of mold or dust on his shoes, as if whoever had created him would never be forgiven. He often asked me questions interrogation-style, baiting me so I would cry. He wanted me to say that he was right, that his ancestors who hung like gloomy decorations on our walls were unparalleled rarities in the world and that he was, like his relatives, a man who could never be replicated. He wanted me to be thankful every day that I had found him, and to see my father as an enemy who'd warped my girlhood and development. He tried to ensure I would never be in league with my father's deviant ideas.

Sami always asked me about my father's Christian friends, what rituals they practiced and if we'd eaten in their homes. I told him about winter visits we'd made to the Bcharré region in the mountains. I described how we could reach out to touch the snow that we saw all around us, how it filled the silent air with peace. He would listen eagerly to what I was saying, like a little boy. But then his mood would flip, as if suddenly remembering that he wasn't supposed to be at all impressed by anything related to my past.

"Did he sit in his office all day long?"

"Yes."

"Did you sit with him?"

"No, but sometimes I would sneak in there."

"Why?"

"To see what he was reading."

"Do you think reading is meaningful?"

"Sort of."

"He didn't ever try to pray?"

"No."

"He didn't go to the mosque on Friday?"

"No, he never went."

"And your mother?"

"I think that she was more religious than him."

"Did he forbid her from praying?"

"No, but she never told him that she liked to pray."

"Did people ever visit him?"

"No, very rarely."

"And what about you, did you see his friends?"

"No, why do you keep on talking about my father's life?"

"Because people in the neighborhood say a lot of things about him."

"But you know that they aren't true."

"Religious men don't lie, and they don't like him."

Before I could express how annoyed I was at what he was saying, he told me to come close to him and make love. He knew that our conversation had stripped me of absolutely everything—the arguments I used to defend my family, my religiosity or lack of it, my body, my very existence. It became easier for him to seize and possess me because I was too weakened to resist.

Every time he came inside of me after similar conversations, I felt like he was stealing me right from my father's lap and turning me into an obedient plaything. The only feeling I experienced when our bodies came together was that I was a black hole, a woman with no scent, a stick broken off a tree branch, lying on the ground for people to tread on as they passed.

CHAPTER 10

Sami moved nimbly through the alleys in Tripoli's Zahriyeh neighborhood to reach the small apartment near the Al-Mir Bakery where he'd spent his early childhood. Like so many boys, he had loved playing soccer. From the time his little feet could kick a ball he wanted to score goals. He used to wait on the street corner for his friends and they would all walk together to the big pitch behind the Carmelite monastery school where he'd had his first lessons. There was no trace of a female presence in the "Italian school," as it was called back then. It was strange that a boy who'd grown up in an atmosphere of peace and harmony between Muslims and Christians later came to prefer social segregation.

It was an all-boys school, where crude adolescent conversations met sports and competition. They were immersed in a world with no females, who in their minds could only be a movie star, the girl next-door, or a local woman reputed to be a beauty. The older boys met up on the weekends to go to the Piccadilly Cinema and watch whatever films were showing.

Before Sami and his family left the old neighborhood behind and moved to Azmi Street, he failed grade six in middle school. He has yet to recover from this defeat. Clutching his report card, he started jogging down the street as if he were the only one there. Everyone on the sidewalk followed him with their eyes. He burst into the house, gasping for air and giving his mother a shock. One of the neighbors heard her shriek and came rushing over. She had to find a way to defuse the situation as well as an excuse for her son's disastrous mark before the word "failure" stuck to him. So, she shouted loudly, "Oh, my son, this is because you are a Muslim boy studying with Christian monks. I've been telling your father to change your school!" She turned to her neighbor and exclaimed, "You see, Imm Adel, they failed my boy!"

His mother wrapped him in her arms, and without even bothering to see what other marks he'd gotten, whispered in his ear, "Soon we will put you in a school with people like us, and they'll value you more there."

My husband told me about this incident one day when we were passing by the big Protestant evangelical church at the top of the street on the way to the Mansouri mosque. His eyes shifted from the dome of the mosque and the cross on the church while recounting his story. He talked about how he hated his old school, had grown distant from his classmates, and only met them to beat them in soccer.

He dribbled the ball, setting his sights on the net so he could win. When he lost, he turned into a beast, refusing to communicate with his friends at all. When he'd return home, his mother would put ice cubes on his bruises and praise him as if he'd won. If he ever got discouraged by his losses, she would tell him that his kicks were so powerful they'd uprooted the grass, and next time the ball wouldn't dare escape him.

More often than not, I hoped that my husband would stay away from me. I couldn't stand the weight of his body on top of me. Whenever I felt his saliva on my breasts, I was overwhelmed by a desire to vomit. Since I was in that idealistic-realistic world, I knew I was close to rock bottom. The closer he got to me physically, the more and more distant from me he felt.

In his face, I saw men whose lust vibrated in their necks— their saliva dripping as they waited for a widow to stop dancing so they could make a move on her. When he put his left hand on my slender waist, it was like everyone had stopped dancing, the blood rising to their heads and boiling over in anger, tongues hanging from their panting mouths. I used to dream that my bed would gradually get bigger and bigger until it swallowed me up and I disappeared. But no bed ever took me in, and he had no mercy on me. I would simply close my eyes and try to disappear into another world until those minutes had passed. When I woke up from the coma I was in, I would go back to trying to figure out ways to evade him and never have to sleep with him ever again.

Once he pinned my hands down on the bed and suddenly let them go. He brushed back strands of hair dangling in my face and stared at me. I looked for a place I could escape to between the ceiling and the cherry-wood wardrobe. He caressed my face saying, "You are so tasty, my wife." I escaped from his grasp and ran into the bathroom. I bolted the door and looked in the mirror. My features assaulted me. Everything turned into Me, even the toilet paper roll hanging in its elegant silver container, the laundry basket that held two pairs of his dirty underwear, even the toilet. All of this became "Me."

I touched myself. I took a slightly dirty satin nightgown out of the washing machine to rub over my body. I leaned my head against the wall and saw a place full of grief. The things looked like me, not only because I had transformed into a plastic box or a porcelain wall, but because they were also trapped and unable to escape.

He knocked on the door. "What's going on? Did you fall asleep in there, Sahar?"

I asked him to use the other bathroom. He grumbled, and I followed the sound of his footsteps to be sure he was far away, and that more than one door separated me from him, even though the extra distance was only a couple of meters. I looked at my wristwatch. Its hands were frozen in place; time was standing still inside me, dying without moving.

As my relationship with Sami began to worsen, I realized that time dies within us until we crumble into mere ashes. Life is not simply a matter of the planets being in orbit or being engrossed in daily affairs. Rather, life is the minutes we feel pulsating in our hearts; it's what we hold within us, what flows into us. Life is the moments when we are in love, when pleasure fills us up and overflows from our bodies and souls. All of these places cramped me. Death engulfed me until I was suffocating and unable to swallow myself. I desperately needed to breathe, but I couldn't find any air.

I turned on the tap to regulate my body temperature. I felt fleeting pleasure standing under the shower, as if my flattened breasts had suddenly returned to where they were supposed to be, becoming erect once again after the heinous torment sucking at them and destroying them. The scent of rape and death hung in the quivering air of the room.

The water slipped over my body like drops of rain falling on a parched sidewalk, or dewdrops clinging to the stem of a flower.

I wondered when this living hell would end and I might find a bit of freedom, even a little bit.

My husband called out to me again, saying we were late to go and see his family and the children had already gone ahead of us. I wrapped myself up in a towel, wondering why I had to accompany him on these silly visits, which sucked me dry. I always felt very uncomfortable at them. I could already hear the voices of his parents and his whole family. I didn't like them as I had at the beginning of our relationship. So often, I felt like I didn't like anyone who connected me to my real life. I fled into my imaginary world, searching for new faces.

I used to conjure up people so I could secretly laugh at and make fun of the people around me. This is how my life had always happened—inside of me. My relationships with other people have always been tumultuous and problematic in ways that I could never understand. Because I had such a powerful desire to be close with others, if I hit the smallest of roadblocks, I would retreat into my shell like a turtle does to keep safe from any danger.

But things are different now. I don't even want to see my mother and I've avoided visiting her. Since I told her that my husband hits me, and I chose to keep this a secret from my father, I started feeling that she didn't love me anymore. So as not to make things harder on her, I started asking myself if she really needed to be the one to protect me. Shouldn't I stand up and defend myself?

I dithered a lot before telling her that my husband was beating me. In fact, I didn't expect her support, but I wanted to somehow blame her for the situation I'd ended up in.

"So, like how often does he hit you?"

"Well, once a month or every two weeks, depending on how angry he is."

"And what do you do?"

"I don't do anything. I stay quiet."

"Your luck turned out like mine, poor girl."

"I'm not like you, Mom. I'm telling you because I can't stay quiet."

"Why don't you tell your dad?"

"I don't have the heart. I am afraid he'll get upset. He didn't want me to get married in the first place."

"Listen, my girl, all men are like that. They want to be big and strong, and, when they can, they take their bad moods out on women."

"Why do women put up with it?"

"God made us this way, to put up with stuff. Look how we manage to carry babies in our bellies. He chose women to help him in creation."

"If God loves women so much, why did he only have male prophets?"

"Woah, shut it, that's enough… Don't blaspheme! Look where your father's unbelief has led us."

In those moments I didn't know if my mother's lack of empathy was indicative of her pain, her reality, or simply her indifference to me. I was trying to understand the way she looked at me. Did she feel vindicated because I ended up like her? Or did she simply not know a different reality for women? The only thing in the world she did know was the bedroom she slept in with my father, always alone. Years went by, she passed thirty, then forty, she was closing in on fifty and she looked the same. The only thing that changed was her age.

CHAPTER 11

I locked the door to my room so I could put my clothes on in peace. I took a dress out of the wardrobe randomly. I reached out to pick up my underwear from the drawer and I felt his hand wrap around my waist. I removed it from my body angrily, and asked him, "Didn't you just say we were late? Let me get dressed." Since I realized that an angry look wouldn't frighten him, I pasted a weak smile on my lips, exposing my perplexity and panic. I kissed his forehead with exaggerated sweetness and asked him to leave the room while I got dressed.

Sami stood at the door and watched me putting my clothes on. He asked, "Do you love me, Sahar?"

I tried to evade the question by telling him that he'd chosen an inopportune moment for a romantic question. I tried to convince him that I was busy thinking about the children, and whether or not they'd already eaten. I rambled on about our son Tareq and how he was eating too much chocolate.

I tried to keep my voice neutral and not sound agitated. I moved my lips quickly and involuntarily. My heart fell right to the pit of my stomach and then rose back up to lodge itself in my throat. This is my tell; this is when it becomes obvious when I am lying, haunted by timeless noise.

Sami shut me up and repeated his question. I stared at the edge of the bed. I searched for a creative way to equivocate successfully. Many words of disgust and loathing that a woman might say to a man flowed through my mind. All of the irritating feelings that I was unable to express poured into my heart. Whenever he touched any part of my body, it rejected and refused him. I felt nauseated when he kissed me, and by his voice, which I could no longer tolerate. His surplus of affection only suffocated me, as did his non-stop knowledge of all things and his endless attempts to dominate me and control my life. I often thought about the lottery tickets I bought at the beginning of each week: I must make a fortune so that my children and I can escape this man.

All of these thoughts were piling up in my head as I tried to come up with an appropriate response to Sami's question. I stopped staring at the edge of the bed and lifted my head. Realizing that lying was inevitable, I pushed down all of those images and said, "Of course, I love you." He smiled cunningly, a merchant who knows he's just sealed a counterfeit deal that multiplied his earnings. I realized bitterly that we were hypocrites. Of course, I love you, Sami. Can the victim escape the love of the executioner? This is how my husband and I turned into silent enemies, brought together by a shared life in which everything was separate.

Sami drove the car calmly. Sitting in the passenger seat, I gazed out the window, my face pressed up against the glass. I started convincing myself that I was a magical being with the gift of extraordinary strength, who could fight against rejection and the despicable Self who tried to dampen my spirit. This fantasy would take me away from the man I was bound to. I also embraced lofty thoughts, like suicide in the arms of a man I rejected, because the city, its streets, the Great Mansouri Mosque, whose dome reached the sky, stated that my happiness is here. My mother also says my life is here. The voice of pleasure inside me is an evil demon from hell that God sent to test my patience.

I saw the specter of Shaykh Bilal in the alleys we passed through. I heard his sarcastic laughter and reckoned he was saying, "I am sending you to hell because of your base thoughts and your desire to wear red shoes. I will burn you all in hellfire, you and your father and all the communists in the land." I felt like he had kicked me in the eye, blinding me, leaving me gaping at the feet of an angel and pleading for mercy. Then Shaykh Bilal stuck his full lips on the angel's sword and cut off my head before throwing me in the grave half dead, half alive.

I viewed Sami as a mere fly buzzing around like an evil omen. I hoped that he would disappear like a block of incense burning under the blazing sun. To me, this was exactly like the savages who bound their dead before throwing them into the grave to keep them from getting out and turning into ghosts.

A perpetual desire to hold onto something was always with me, whether it was the glass of the car window, or windowpanes in the house, or the edge of the bed that I clutched in terror, or the kitchen chair that I sat on for hours without moving. I was like a car with its hood removed, a fragile yellow leaf blasted by frost. My soul was restless and I felt like I was everywhere all at once. I wandered through labyrinths that had been within me since birth. Screams surrounded me and gave me voice. It was as if this Me had to be my prior Me. She was born before I had a body and an existence, before I was a living being. It had invaded me at the beginning of my thirties to tell me, "Now you have to be me. You are not you, you are me." Just as a hermit vows to live for God, I became the property of an involuntary force that I could not touch or see, but whose every detail I could feel.

I started wondering if Sami knew the extent of the turbulence inside of me or that the vibrations of my soul were wandering around in an environment totally alien to him? I looked at his face carefully. He made odd movements while walking, thrusting his shoulder out, puckering his lips unevenly, and strutting about. All of these flaws became striking to look at. I searched in his hazel eyes and light brown skin for something that would set him apart from others and did not find it. Sami had no distinguishing features. His reedy voice disgusted me; it was incompatible with his large body and the oversized birthmark on his forehead. When I looked at him, I could see nothing else. His entire face would turn into the birthmark.

I was perpetually afraid that I would die standing on his threshold. For me, this became a symbol of the ending of all endings, the endings of dreams and desires, of life or clinical death. His bizarre way of walking, his large, hooked nose, his laughing eyes all spelled out death to me. The few minutes during which he would have sex with me were no less than the end of my body.

He parked the car in front of the large iron gates and we got out. Tareq came running toward me, he threw himself in my arms and pulled me to him powerfully. I kissed his cheek and asked him, "Have you eaten yet, habibi?" He nodded and kissed me back, falling into my arms. He took a ball from the trunk of the car and ran free, far away. His cousins called out to him, wanting to play with him, and he waved at me. I smiled weakly, wishing I could be as calm as he was.

He had an oval-shaped head and walked with confidence. He was plump and handsome. His voice was unique. His eyes were not green but jet-black. Unlike his sister, his looks took nothing from his father's side. My daughter, Dunya, looked a lot like her father in her facial features, though she was much sweeter and gentler in character.

The day she was born, I went to the hospital in the morning with moderate pain and cramping. There was a woman scream-ing in the room they put me in. Her husband wasn't there. Her mother was with her and stayed right next to her, listening to her screams. I didn't know if I would ever forget this woman's stern features. She looked at her daughter and implored her doctor to move her from the labor room to the delivery room so he could finish quickly.

Her movements were involuntary, like a machine in motion. Doesn't a mother feel sympathy or empathy with her daughter's pain? I asked myself if my image of mothers was too idealized compared to the reality. I asked the nurse to give me a painkiller and refused to let anyone in to see me until I'd given birth. Only Sami came in periodically to check on me.

When the time to deliver approached, I asked him to stay near me. He didn't seem tense or anxious, and indeed he liked being there, in control of things. Whenever the pain increased in intensity, I squeezed his hand tightly. I remember that I loved him in that moment. Perhaps not a fierce and overwhelming love that shakes a person to the core, but I felt an affection for him, mixed with compassion. I had not yet been completely alienated from him; his extreme and exaggerated behavior was still under control. Sami's violence against me didn't intensify until I started protesting against the things I didn't like.

The doctor didn't allow anyone into the delivery room with me that day. I heard Dunya's first cry and looked right at her. She was born with her eyes open. The doctor grabbed her, turned her over, and held her upside down. I screamed in terror and he reassured me that this was how things were done. Sami and my family members were waiting outside. They took Dunya into another room. Everyone gathered around me to congratulate me, but sheer exhaustion made me want to simply surrender to a deep sleep.

When Dunya was born, this increased the number of people my husband and I shared between us. But the bond that should have brought me closer to him and made me feel his tenderness was illusory. It was as if children were not merely the product of relations between a man and a woman but an integrated embodiment of that relationship. If the chasm between them grows, they become it.

He stayed next to me throughout that night. He slept on the bed beside mine. I woke up at around midnight, famished. I ate a little chocolate that I had in my purse and the nurse brought Dunya so I could breastfeed her. I held my baby for the first time. I cradled this tiny body in my arms—a hungry moving mouth and two eyes that could not see—groping for her life from me.

Sami didn't wake up. Nothing woke him, but I kept hoping he would wake. I wanted those things that you see in films to come true, like when the man stays next to his wife and helps her with all the little things. I was dreaming all along, I sought out an ideal relationship, perfection in everything I did. I rearranged my clothes several times a day. I dusted the furniture in my house every day and I spent hours polishing the crystal that I always kept orderly. The image—the reflection that connected me to the Other—had to be kept free of any impurities or defects.

I could not bear the idea of disappointing others or that they would look at me and think that I was not a perfect woman. I didn't know what I wanted to be, and I didn't have any goal in life except for Sami and the children to be happy. I wanted the people around me to be satisfied with me, and I didn't always express clearly what was going on inside my mind for fear that they wouldn't like what I was thinking, just as they didn't like what my father thought.

I agreed with Sami when he criticized his coworkers, even though I didn't find the things he said to have much bearing on reality. Now I realize that I was escaping into his way of thinking for fear of being myself. I lived in his identity, not because I didn't have one, but because I was afraid of expressing it. I wanted our image to remain coherent, regardless of the cracks than had begun showing. A person looking between the lines would only be able to see a house and a garden with calm, harmonious colors. This portrait looked normal from the outside. It was as if I—who was fully aware of its inner pain—had struck an unannounced deal: we would keep each other's secrets hidden.

Everyone in his family always gathered together to eat lunch. Their voices mingled with the clatter of spoons against dishes, hands reached out to take pieces of bread. Sami would eat and his mother would keep dishing out more food for him. This is how it always was; she spoiled him excessively. She treated him like a little boy and always made me feel that he was better than I was, and that I was no good at looking after him. The desire to rule over their family ran through her veins, the rotten blood of people who thought they were superior to others. All of them were surprisingly amazing—the father, the mother, the children, the grandchildren. And there I was, the outsider, who had no place among all the glory that was their family's patrimony.

I know exactly how things happen in this picture—the long, boring Sunday comes to an end. We get in the car and go back home. I put the children to bed and Sami and I watch a movie together. We go to bed. He tries to have sex with me. Fearing the quarrel that will result if I refuse, I relent. Maybe he won't hit me. I don't want to wake the children.

CHAPTER 12

At the beginning of my thirties, I decided to adopt a new look and started wearing clothes with unusual designs. I became obsessed with buying shoes, perfume, and underwear. I started caring a lot about art, especially musical performances. I became increasingly interested in knowing more about religion, so I started reading books on Buddhism and Hinduism and thinking about the soul. No one had ever really talked to me about such things before.

I always felt like God was something strange in my life—as if I were a rope being pulled on at both ends. The first side encouraged me to confess to him without knowing him, the second to deny him, but also without getting to know him. The only time I felt close to faith was during a childhood conversation with the neighbor's daughters after their mother had died of cancer.

It was the story of Zeinab—the Mother of the Girls as she was known in the neighborhood. After she'd given birth to three daughters in a row, her husband brought home a second wife in the hope that he would have a male son and heir to complete his manhood. Zeinab lived with this humiliation because of her background. She gathered her daughters around the fireplace in the winter and told tales of princesses and houris who bathed in golden water, while she roasted potatoes and chestnuts and sang beautiful songs as rain showers beat against the windowpanes.

She did her very best to please her husband. She was eager to serve him hot meals and constantly sought out his approval even when he was shouting in her face. Neither her hot food nor her elegance was enough to intercede with him on her behalf. She couldn't atone for her guilt about not giving birth to the crown prince but only three mere girls. She was haunted by the premonition that he would marry a second wife who would ruin her, as his mother threatened that he would, until one day he did.

One time, Zeinab revolted against her fate as a prisoner. She cursed at her husband's snippiness and she let his food get cold. She took off her abaya and banged her head against the wall.

"I have had enough humiliation, it's enough!" she shouted like a madwoman, repeating this over and over again urgently. "Didn't you enter me when I was carrying these girls in my uterus? Didn't you plant your seed in my belly? Enough humiliation!" she screamed at the top of her lungs.

She banged her head and muttered incomprehensibly. She opened the doors to the house, and when the doors were open wide, she tried to run away. But her destiny was simply to be stuck there, what luck! Her husband, Hajj Massad, then took off his leather belt and showed no mercy. He shoved her to the ground and brutalized her feet, head, and back. What better place to rid himself of his anger than on the Mother of the Girls' body?

Zeinab was bedridden for the next three days, moaning and crying. She knew that when she recovered and gained consciousness that she would experience an even greater humiliation. She was condemned to be a slave, imprisoned once again in order to learn how to accept her enslavement without any protest.

After three days, no doubt she spent three more days being crushed under his feet. She washed them with her tears, kissed them, and bowed down before his tyranny and power. The Hajj enjoyed every minute of this punishment. He would have let her spend the rest of her life apologizing and excusing herself without anyone knowing how miserable and overburdened she really was.

"I apologize and I don't know why. I'm bearing the brunt of crimes I didn't commit," she would tell my mother and then carry on, "But it's OK, Souad. Everything I do is so I can take care of my girls. I'm really worried about them."

Our neighbor was exhausted by her oppression. My mother soothed her wounds with intimacy. She tried to make things easier for her; she encouraged her to be patient and to pray for some relief. But her supplications failed and she died sick and miserable. The two sisters wept a lot over their mother's death, and everyone shouted at them to stop wailing. Then their little sister Salma came and told them that they shouldn't cry because her girlfriend had assured her that God in heaven wouldn't beat her.

"He won't hit her, don't worry," the youngest sister said.

But her daughters were afraid that we wouldn't care for or respect the Mother of the Girls after watching her suffer for so long. They needed to hear more than just "Mom is OK." They wanted to know that she had found her salvation with God. They decided to pray to him every day so that he would respond and return her to them. They spoke about God innocently, in a way I had never heard before. They pinned their hopes on their mother being returned to them.

I would never forget this story or the sight of the girls' features distorted with pain. I started secretly wondering if God would ever actually hear us and respond.

God was silence and serenity. You couldn't speak about him, or speculate about his daily life, or be his friend. You had no right to debate this. Only infidels believed that you could communicate with God. Only unbelievers wake up in the morning and look around for him so they can have a chat with him and say good morning, or even good night. I often thought that I was a bad person and that I deserved the misfortunes that befell me because I was in a state of perpetual doubt. I had an equivocal relationship with faith, tainted by panic and many barriers.

My relationship with my husband was really what kept me from worshipping and praying, because I found it unbearably false to deal with what is supposed to be beautiful and elegant. According to his behavior, religion was a means of competition or a way to negate the Other, to be condescending and arrogant. It was the trade in values he would extrapolate depending on his need. I started to understand why my father cursed religious men, especially given the miserable state of the city. They only ever used their power and authority to tear things down, rather than to build them up. They tightened their grip on the youth, taming and training them to be satisfied with the bare minimum so they could never dream of change.

It was not only my relationship with men of religion that was complicated, but also my relationship with all of my surroundings. What aroused the most anger in me were the falsehoods I saw everywhere I looked. It seemed that no one was really living, but rather just pretending to live, that they were born into ready-made metal molds and preferred to remain inside them, too slack and spineless to leave their predefined boxes. I asked myself if they, like me, had found homes in imaginary other lives, or if their desire was simply dead.

Are we all unconsciously driven by the influence of tradition—what is good and bad, right and wrong, halal and haram? Or do some people benefit from a life-versus-death-based lifestyle because it promotes and even justifies inertia? Are peace and contentment a blessing under which we live in safety, or are they a curse that kills any spark within us, convincing us that we do not have enough to face up to life?

The thing that pained me the most were expressions like "C'est la vie," or "We have to accept our fate," or "What can we do?" I no longer know if realism is really our best option or simply the product of successive disappointments and losses, the result of previous dreams and desires that brought nothing but woe.

On city streets and in people's homes, the youth had no dreams beyond finding a job to go to in the morning, so they could come back home, have an afternoon nap, and spend the evening visiting friends and family or just stay in the house glued to the television screen. When I stayed awake during afternoon naptime, I felt like I was living on a small planet where everyone else was asleep. My attempts to fall into a deep slumber were unsuccessful, and I hated sleeping even at night because I had an irrepressible desire for life that I could see escaping from me.

How did I go from being a woman full of idealism to being a filthy and unfaithful one?

How did the strands of my secret life unravel and escape from me like rosary beads falling to the ground? I no longer know myself. How did I find my Self and where did I lose her? None of this means anything any longer since I can't really undo any of it. I can't disappear and I can't escape from life. I acquired the golden rule slowly, only to find comfort in the forbidden, the lowest depths into which I fell with much disappointment and desperation.

In the darkness, I imagined myself as someone with a sensitive disposition. Others saw this as excessive immorality. But I tried to maintain a photogenic outward appearance that I derived from these Others, because the only thing I felt for my society was an obsession with how they looked.

After long months and years of marriage during which this state of nothingness took on a new form, connected to a painful reality that had nothing to do with what my imagination had woven, I was bound to step out of the daily prison where I was shackled, and evolve into something else.

When nobody was paying attention, I made drawings of the interior design of houses and kept them stored in a little locked box. I wasn't able to find real work in my field, however, because Sami refused to let me do freelance work, i.e., anything other than a regular 9-to-5 job. He also rejected the idea of drawing and design, which he considered a waste of time. All I could find was a job with an insurance company doing routine administrative work for a paltry salary.

I couldn't refuse it, though, because I desperately needed to interact with the world, in any little way, so that I could live my life. I would walk to the building where I worked, near home, and started taking long strolls under the cloudy skies. I breathed in the scent of asphalt and watched the cars speed by.

Every day I passed a giant tree that was planted between two bits of sidewalk, and I would watch droplets of water slide down its leaves and settle on its branches. This suffused me with serenity, and the hope that one day I could touch a branch and live in a giant tree, without all the fuss of thoughts and feelings and without the nothingness that kept me awake in bed for long, sleepless nights. Though sometimes I would run joyfully through the streets, I knew how deeply disappointed and alienated from life I actually was. The only thing I really wanted—with the same passion that other people seek out wealth and money—was to walk the streets, with their polluted air, disgusting smells, and the noisy bustle of living, breathing people.

I would laugh to myself while walking down the street, causing people in the crowd to look at me as if I were deranged. I had no reason to be so happy, but I wanted to stop passersby, look them in the eye, and tell them that I'd seen them in my dreams and had made an interior design plan for their houses. I wanted to tell them that I'd always wanted to belong to them, but I could not. I was forbidden from being in the world by first my father, then my mother, and now my husband.

I swear that I could have continued the conversation and that things had gotten better—now that I could go out to my job, window-shop, and buy underwear, perfume, or a new dress for myself.

Sometimes I'd start conversations with people begging on the street and ask them about where they came from and how they had landed in their situation. They only put up with my overzealous questioning because they knew they'd get some money out of it at the end. Perhaps deep down they were thinking about how empty this crazy lady must be. When I noticed that time was running short, I'd scramble back to work in a hurry. When I reached the door I'd calm down, walk in, and move around the room with my feet close together, wearing the smile of a sedate and sober woman.

I completed my work quietly, contemplating all these insurance contracts—life, car, home. I asked myself if we really needed all these papers to be safe and secure. And if we did, would these be enough to help us find that almost-impossible-to-find inner peace?

When I dealt with clients, I felt an overwhelming desire to laugh sarcastically. They seemed to be angling to guarantee themselves life and permanence, not immunity from accidents. Can you have immunity against memories? Against nothingness? Against rejection? Against doubt? Are they satisfied with knowing that if they were to die in an accident, there would be a positive material impact on their family?

A person who knows the cruelty and ugliness of life needs guarantees—and a lot of them. They can't have them, but their children can, and they want to spare them misery and prevent them from hitting rock bottom. Perhaps a wife won't find anyone to provide for her if her husband dies. The irony was watching people scrambling to strike a bargain about what will come after death, while still alive.

Perhaps most of them were like me, plagued by a permanent feeling of danger and feeling that their existence may be distorted by what awaited them in the beyond. This is why they rush to inoculate themselves with an insurance policy. But who fixes broken souls? Who can insure against the devastation and sorrow that death leaves behind? Who could insure me against the nothingness that inhabits me?

If we had even the slightest ability to love, we wouldn't need all of these guarantees. We would be content with some pure affection from the Other, rather than the fear that has been cultivated within us from our first breath. Perhaps the opposite is more common: we need the love of the Other in order to boost our Selves and survive our feelings of nothingness. Therefore, we burn many bridges and trample over anything that might interfere with our existence just to try to affirm it. Killing the soul is merely an outdated attempt to repair and glorify the body. Likewise, killing the body is merely an outdated attempt to convince the soul it is ideal. This is the abyss into which my mother fell.

CHAPTER 14

I wished that I could stay in Rabih's arms for the rest of my life. I wanted our time together to never end, to be able to carry the feeling of ecstasy inside me like a souvenir of him. I wanted to trap his scent in my pores to help me get through the days yet to come. My desires felt out of reach. There was a difficult road to travel and I did not know where it ended. But I did know that it was my own desire.

I believed the voice that told me to love because it came from deep inside of me. It's the voice that wraps around my heart where Rabih is. Thinking about him for hours at a time is pure pleasure. I can experience extreme pleasure by just getting lost in his eyes. As soon as I dissolve into his arms, I even feel my fugitive soul returning to me.

Rabih asked me to take off my clothes and I loved it when he gazed at me naked. He used to tell me that he wanted to discover my body. Even though he'd already memorized all of its details, he always made me feel that he was looking at it for the very first time. Something beautiful was happening to me, something forbidden, shameless, and strange. It was as if I were moving to a lush garden, away from prying eyes. Light carefully spilled into the room and I was able to see empty circles and squares on the walls, and the white wire extending behind the bed. Simply standing naked like this made me more attentive to detail. It made my senses more capable of detecting Rabih's body from afar. It was as if this distance between our two bodies gave our souls an opportunity to make love in the sweetest possible way.

My long black hair flowed down over my shoulders. Rabih's gaze upon me made me a woman at once mad and subdued, calm and angry, who loves beauty and life above all. I gazed back at him and was invaded by a deep desire to be close to him. I wanted him in those moments, and I know that he wanted me. He pushed me down onto the sofa. He rained kisses all over my body. Just like in my dreams, I was falling from a high place, suspended between earth and sky. I didn't know how my body fell back onto the bed, nor how it touched reality, but I heard no noise or crash. I fell into a winged soul whom the universe had granted peace and calm.

In my imagination I saw a woman stretched out wide, on a mysterious horizon, almost as wide as the sea, arms encircling her head. The wave reached so high that she cried out and embraced the salty water to bathe in everything that was not herself and reach its true, mysterious depths. She lifted her legs to embrace an unknown face, beaded with sweat. She opened her legs and they were joined together with conscious, painful force, so the face and body became one.

Like any wonderful thing in life, it had to end. Reality called. I got dressed, put on my sunglasses, and left the building feeling neither embarrassed nor afraid. My forbidden love was entirely right. It was as if without this passion, I would not be able to find my balance and I would lose my way.

I don't know where all my courage came from when it came to infidelity. Perhaps it came from thinking about the consequences of things or the despair in not thinking about them. This despair causes my deepest Self to say, "Let it be." I was like a criminal pursued by the police, who throws himself in the water when he reaches the sea and drowns while attempting to save himself.

Death didn't frighten me at all. I experienced it every minute I was with my husband, but I was also thirsty for life and threw myself right into it. I left women who weep noisily, scratch their faces, and pull out their hair behind me. I was able to see myself leading a procession. Young women who saw us would shout out, throw their handkerchiefs away, dumping them where fear resided, and follow me to the edge of the precipice. I was leading this procession, calling out, "Let the women scream!" And this was true not just of young women as fresh as new apples, but also of fully grown, mature women, sweet as honey. These were the women stored up inside every man, the ones society had forbidden to be let out.

My exposure to humiliation and indignity in my marriage made me ponder why I worked only to satisfy others. It made me reflect on what I actually wanted. Images of the false idols surrounding me—my parents and girlfriends— floated through my mind. Many faces passed by, besieging me from all sides. And then the voices. The voice of my mother saying that a woman has to control her emotions so she can maintain her social status. The voice of my girlfriend who knew her husband was having sex with other women but who assures me that he'll come back to her for good, eventually. The voice of a woman's dignity colliding with things left in ruins, saying she doesn't care as long as her material needs are fulfilled. She has a margin of freedom now, one that allows her to receive visitors but also demands that she spend hours on social obligations that add nothing to her life. I often wonder if these women had abandoned their desires. Perhaps they weren't really looking for love, just some peace and quiet.

CHAPTER 15

Within about a year, I had gained both a lover and a friend. I'd never had either one before. Rabih was one of the customers at the insurance company where I worked. The first time I saw him, he lowered his head and looked at me as though we were in our own private scene in a film. I handed him back his papers feeling confused, as if my hands were stretching out only to meet his. He told me I was beautiful. My response was rough and even a bit harsh; I acted as if I hadn't heard what he said. Still, I couldn't help but look at him kindly, even if it might be taken as somewhat inappropriate. When he noticed I was wearing a wedding ring, he asked me if I was married. I nodded, and he kept talking to me, though my answers were brief. He asked me if I was happy and I didn't respond. A terrifying silence filled the room. I saw a woman stuck in quicksand, everything swirling around her. She was deaf, distant, unconnected to anything. Then everything around me disintegrated and liquefied. He repeated his question. As the world around me crumbled, I once again became visible.

In all my thirty years of existence, no one had ever asked me if I was happy. I didn't know how to respond. I started thinking about all the women who weren't happy and whether they had lovers. It seemed to me that these women had particular features, similar faces. They carried big purses containing everything they needed—the tools of their infidelity. That day, I started wondering if there was something in my features that revealed my misery. Perhaps it was in the way I walked, how I sat, or even my hand movements.

I started imagining a woman standing on a sidewalk holding a shopping bag, her purse tucked under one arm, staring out at the street in front of her. It seemed she'd gotten tired of waiting, or maybe she was never actually waiting for anyone. I thought about my mother and wondered if she had ever thought about a man other than my father. As I'd gotten older, I'd started thinking about her as a woman and not just as my mother.

On my way home, I noticed some people around me holding glasses and wearing fancy clothes. Two men with lackluster features stopped in front of me. Then Rabih appeared from afar, sitting tall atop a purebred horse. I waved at him and motioned for him to come over to where I was, but he passed by without returning my greeting, leaving me to throw myself on the ground.

I realized that I was an adversary of the woman who appeared in my fantasies. She caused me pain because she was overcome with desire, making me fight against my Self until she robbed me of it. But she was much more beautiful than me. Warm and fresh. I used to see her coming toward me slowly, opening her arms to invite me into her soft, distant bosom. There was a light within her that filled her eyes with tears. Instead of uniting with her, my lonely, jealous body pushed her far away. She screamed for me to come back to her. She begged me. So I buried her beneath the earth so she couldn't move anymore. She would have to close her eyes and stay there alone, completely still.

I remained resentful for the whole rest of the night, until I saw dawn rise through my small bedroom window. The morning light cast a shadow over my husband's face. He was like two different men to me. I felt an infinite desire to cause him pain that night. I held and squeezed my breasts against each other, then got up to walk around the room, smoked a cigarette and cried.

I knew that the panic I experienced was a mixture of fear, remorse, and guilt for being with someone who exercised such complete control over me. He deprived me of my sovereignty, dignity, self-esteem, and almost of my very mind. But my desire to escape, despite how wounded I was, was a sign that I was not completely destroyed. I did maintain some measure of dignity deep within me. In fact, I was not a victim of deception but of my own will. I spent several years subordinate and obedient to an authoritarian man. When I regained consciousness, this fact sent me into a state of inner rage and despair.

I stood there waiting for the return of the woman I'd expelled from my Self. I could see two shadows from a silent film scene before me. One held the other close, comforting her. Then they exchanged positions. I later imagined the city, comparing it to how I imagined houses, streets, and roads. In reality it had no colors. Everything was black and white. "Colors on paper," said the first woman's shadow. The second woman's shadow told her to wash her eyes with water so she could see colors. But if the first was out of earshot, the second would repeat the same question, "Who has the answers? Who has the answers?"

Perhaps it is the similarity between Hala and one of the women in my imagination that drew me closer to her. I had contemplated her a great deal from afar. She had a full figure, brown hair, round eyes, and was constantly in motion. I observed her taut skin and stark features, her gracious way of dealing with other people as well as her simplicity and impulsiveness. Hala was not conventionally beautiful, but small things about her, like her perceptive gaze, made her luminous. She had a smile that made you feel you could overcome all of the world's hardships and cruelty.

Hala had been widowed since her husband was killed in a traffic accident just two years after they'd gotten together. Fate landed her in a difficult situation: an authoritarian father and a sick child, with no one but her to provide for them. Despite the intense frustration that had stunned her deep in her soul, she insisted on carrying on with her life. When her husband passed away, she felt lifeless with loss. She realized once again that everything was gone.

Hala's eyes lit up when she spoke about her husband, Zeyad. She said she'd never known a man so kind and tender. Then she would always burst into tears. She used to cry, asking me why he'd left her all alone. He didn't know how much she needed him. She'd then laugh bitterly, in pain.

A bee buzzing from flower to flower, Hala stayed sad while keeping busy. Though her grief was somewhat obscured by her outward brassiness, she couldn't hide it from me. This is because I have always confessed my own grief, if only privately, in an attempt to convince myself that my living hell was actually a paradise.

But her sadness didn't stop Hala from singing beautiful songs for others. She was very dignified, at peace with herself, and forgiving. For Hala, the Other was not an absolute entity, but something along the way—not something you get lost in. She always seemed ready for whatever life might bring, not because she was weak, but because she'd come to realize that some things we just endure. We don't always have the ability to change things, but even the worst things may change with time.

Hala said she was trying to wage war on destiny, which brought nothing more than obsolete struggles against the Self. She wanted to stop fighting futile battles and save her strength for more important ones. She tried to create a happy place from nothing. Even though her son had suffered from diabetes since he was tiny, she kept her faith in God.

Her outward signs of faith seemed contraindicated to me, like a kind of miracle. I had been influenced by preconceived notions and stereotypes about men and women believers, like they were all obsessed with wearing appropriate dress or following their constraining daily rituals.

A strong bond formed between Hala and me. We sat together for hours talking about the ways of the world, laughing at the smallest thing. Her son's situation pained me a great deal. Shadi was only ten years old and was severely emaciated from his illness. While playing, he immersed himself in his own imaginary world, but he was like other children in his determination, perseverance, and stubbornness. As a diabetic, he was forbidden to eat candies and pastries, to share in that sacred pleasure of childhood.

Hala's son needed to constantly monitor his glucose levels and was forced to take blood samples to check his sugar. I found the boy very brave for injecting himself with insulin when his mother wasn't there. His bravery in dealing with the disease made our own difficulties seem trivial, as if we adults always gave life's obstacles more weight than they deserved.

CHAPTER 16

As time passed, Sami started beating me again. He would come home from work angry and initiate sex. If I refused, he would grab my hair and throw me on the ground. He would call me a whore and repeat the word until I was in tears. The more I wailed, the more severely he beat me. I absorbed his curses and insults without answering back. My pores widened and absorbed all my agony. I felt like a lowly slut. My body was completely black and blue. After a while, I didn't even bother asking him to stop. I thought I deserved it. In those moments, I lost all feeling in my body, which had separated from my soul and become completely numb.

I remember clearly the first day he beat me. We had just returned from a visit to one of his friends. His friend Yusuf had showered me with compliments. As playful banter, he said, "Your wife is so beautiful, I'm jealous!" Sami laughed and replied, "Your wife has a face as lovely as a full moon." But he looked uncomfortable all evening long, and I asked him if we could leave. On the way home, I asked him what was wrong, and in front of our son, Tareq, he replied, "You were really happy with what Yusuf said, weren't you, bitch?" Not knowing how to answer, I said nothing. One word might ignite his anger, so I absorbed all of his macho jealousy like a sponge.

I didn't think about being unfaithful at that time. In fact, I despised women who engaged in such disgraceful behavior. He wouldn't be jealous if he didn't love me, I figured. My confused mind bubbled over with thoughts. We got home. He called me the ugliest names. He started beating me. No, he wasn't angry. Anger is a transient feeling of discontent; it quickly evaporates without a trace. It was a kind of pain, that's what I liked to believe. When he used to beat me, I would think about him and not myself. It was like a monster had taken over, a monster luring him to eat flesh and drink blood.

The color of Sami's face changed when he stopped hitting me. The skin under his eyes quivered and I could see nothing but his hands in front of my face. I slipped away from him. I shut the bedroom door firmly. I searched for some corner of the house to hide in, not from him but from my Self. Life stopped as I stared at the ceiling. I sat cross-legged, in the corner, afraid, feeling like a mosquito crushed in a man's hand. I was lying on the floor of a bottomless pit. I saw a shadow calling out to me, another woman watching me. I dared not look at her.

All thirty years of my life flashed before my eyes. I was tempted to stop and pay attention, but I started hearing knocking and him ordering me to open the door. The tone of his voice had changed from power into bitterness and disappointment. I realized how much I hated my feet for leading me to the door, how much I detested my cursed, unbroken body.

He squeezed his eyes shut and I wiped the sweat from his forehead. As usual he apologized. He expected me to forget what he had done and forgive him. No, actually, he ordered me to forgive him. I felt my chest heaving and sobbing. I had to swallow it and my Self at the same time. He spoke about Yusuf again. I asked him, "How can you think so badly of me?" He said that he loved me very much and couldn't bear the thought of losing me. He accused me of behaving badly. But then he started listing all the bad things about himself, rather than about me. I started reflecting about how the worst crimes are committed in the name of love and God. Or at least what we think they are.

All I wanted was for him to touch me. But he wanted to feel that he owned me. I ensconced myself in bed and pictured chains hanging off my feet. It was as if someone had handcuffed me and I could only respond to his desires. My body was not mine but his. He was my husband and I had no right to say no to him.

Sami fell asleep and I remained awake for hours, staring at the ceiling. I wondered who could stop this terrible thing happening in my house. Will things stay like this for my entire life? What if I told my father that my husband beat me? My mother always cautioned me not to tell him, to avoid the scandal. But this man must change. I hadn't yet been unfaithful to him. I didn't start cheating on him until my daughter Dunya was four years old. That's when I began to free myself of him. When I got my position at the insurance company, I started owning my own power. I became two women: one whose husband beat her, the other who worked and was productive. The former was not able to be completely who she was, and the latter was unable to use her authority. The feeling that I was slipping out from under his control made him treat me with a measure of kindness. One spring morning, we sat together sipping our morning coffee. He looked at me while I was smoking and said, "You know, women should be more elegant in how they smoke. You put your cigarette out like a lumberjack. You don't just stub it out—you spread ash all around the ashtray. Girls are supposed to blow the smoke out of their noses."

"You're only saying that because you don't like me to smoke."

"No, you don't smoke in a nice way."

"OK, I will practice how you do it."

"Why are you being so rude?"

"I'm not being rude, but I can't find a justification for your objection."

"You are becoming more like your father every day."

"He's my father."

"I'm your husband."

"Yes, I know."

"That's why you have to obey me. Don't ever forget it."

I looked at the cigarette butts lying in the ashtray. I wanted to tell him that I stubbed them out so violently because they represented him and my desire to get him out of my life. The ashes were there to cleanse me of his sins against me as his legal wife.

I learned cruelty from Sami and his family, from their merciless, formal religiosity and their attempt to paint my father as a wounded dog who should be ashamed of his sinful life. But despite his qualities and the pain that he passed down to me, my father somehow represented someone who stood his ground. He followed his conscience despite the powerful backlash of the people around him.

With time, my father traded in his anger for introversion and biting sarcasm. When I looked in his eyes, I realized that he truly was an unbeliever, just as everyone said. He had a nationalist spirit opposed to religion's oppressiveness. He withdrew his gaze when confronted with mine and retreated into his newspaper.

It now occurs to me that the polite, mutual, domestic revulsion my parents had for each other was something trapped between two opposing currents. With grim smiles, they tried to assure us that everything was fine. They exposed many shared secrets about my mother's grief, linked to the specter of her religiosity and my father's aversion to her submission to strange doctrines and beliefs.

The very air that she breathed was charged with panic and dread of the image of the communist man she had chosen to be her life partner. Her libido was like an extermination camp in which every living thing is eradicated, like a sword brandished in the name of conventions, customs, and traditions. I could see plainly where my father had hidden his books at the corner of a remote shelf. Dreams get lost in crowded rows of files. He found a dark hiding place behind other papers.

But other things I saw as I grazed there like a goat made my parents seem more endearing. I saw the office of the company that Sami's family owned, which organized trips for people to go on Hajj. They sold travel necessities, prayer beads, Zamzam water, and pictures of the holy city of Mecca. They ran it as a fraudulent commercial enterprise, convincing the buyers of the quality of their products. I also saw how his mother slapped around the boy who worked for them when he didn't convince clients to buy something.

I watched how their supposedly superior world violated other, lower, worlds. They spent hours brutally criticizing Others, people different from themselves. I observed how they shouted about their grandfather's inheritance, the brothers disagreeing about their shares. They looked at one another with arrogance and hatred after leaving Friday prayers at the Mansouri Great Mosque.

I watched them and wondered if their God could be so bad. But I always pushed any oppositional thoughts out of my mind, for fear that this might land me in some kind of hell, like the one my father was going to burn in for not fulfilling his religious obligations.

CHAPTER 17

With time, I realized that I'd become increasingly abnormal. I remember that, previously, when I'd heard the familiar sound of Sami knocking on the door, I became unbearably impatient because I knew that as soon as he came in, I would drown in inertia. Neither his kisses nor caresses excited me or gave me the pleasure or orgasms that sex was supposed to.

When he opened the main door, a bracing winter breeze seeped into my body. I continually lifted my head, waiting for the coming excitement, never taking my eyes off the hands of the clock, as I knew that he might lose his temper at any moment. When I lay down in bed, I buried my face in the sheets and stretched out as much as I could. The squeak of the bedsprings was my indication that he was done shaving, put on his pajamas, and come to lie down next to me. His proximity was frightening most of the time, but I gradually discovered that this everyday fooling around would grow extremely irritating and tedious.

The more intensely I longed for Rabih, the more distant I felt from my children. The more I missed him, the more constricting the walls of my house became. I felt a lethal loneliness.

I couldn't even hear my children when they were speaking to me. I kept thinking, "What if I just left now? What if I opened that damned wooden door and ran off without turning back?"

My mind wandered as I stared at the door. I dreamed of Rabih breaking down the door with an ax, beating up Sami, and whisking me away. I dreamed that I was holding his hand, fleeing to somewhere I knew no one and no one knew me. It would be a little shack in a remote town where we could make love many times a day. We would fool around without anyone there to inhibit us, and even make love outside, under the trees.

But I would then remember that Rabih wasn't there. There is no torment in this world worse than loneliness. Since I met him, I have thought of nothing else. I no longer cared about the things I used to pay so much attention to before. I closed my eyes and unleashed my imagination. Rabih's tongue melted in my mouth, my breasts swelled in response. His ghost lay next to me in bed, and my body flushed. I had just imagined him coming inside of me, when a voice from the real world said, "Mama, don't go to sleep, I'm really tired."

I jumped up quickly to hug her, and then I burst into tears. I felt so guilty. A few moments earlier, I'd been a mother who didn't want her children, who wanted to be free of them. What caused me so much pain is that it wasn't really the case. I was actually a woman who had children with the wrong man. He was the cause of my vulnerability and misfortune, and he raped me every night.

Dunya asked me why I was crying, and I responded that I was just a bit tired. Her brother soon came too. I embraced the two of them, hugging them both close to me. I wanted to say, "I'm holding you kids close because I want to feel safe like you.

But your father beats me. He's broken everything good inside me and insults me constantly. I'm crying because I'm afraid for the two of you, as well as for myself. I want to spare you my torture, but I can't. I'm crying out my fear, disappointment, and loneliness. I'm afraid I won't be able to give you love ever again."

Grief and panic flowed from my fingers, dripping down out of all of my limbs. I wanted to go back to being a child like my own children and forget all of the pain that had seeped into my pores. I wanted to rid myself of my troubled body, stained as it was with beatings and sin. I hugged them, asking my trembling hands if they were the ones hugging me. I felt the weakness of the being that I am, and its need to draw strength from somewhere even if from a mirage. I remained in this state until all three of us fell asleep in one bed.

CHAPTER 18

The desire to stay in control, and all the associated repercussions of that effort, pushed me to recoil deep inside my Self. It was as if I'd made a pact with myself to hide all of my secrets away in a locked box, but when I tried to recover my treasures, they were hidden from me. The Other would then appear, like a cartoon character or puppet that I move in my mind, whose mask I've removed to expose him. Can I actually see this Other? Or am I pouring myself into him?

Immersing myself in my alternate world is a way of preventing myself from committing sins. I can remain safe this way. But since I'd met Rabih, I experienced the pleasure of sin. I submerged myself in it and forgot everything else. My imagination was no longer certain of the danger of reality, and my fantasies no longer satisfied my desire, which now had a body, feet, and eyes. When he wrapped my shoulders up inside his arms, it felt like he would hold me forever. My very existence diminished and faded into his warm embrace. I became addicted to the feeling of a warm pulse that made dreams possible. As a woman who hailed from a cold dry world and found herself in this fairy tale, living in my reality was all the more difficult.

The wind was cold and had a powerful scent that I breathed right into my pores while smoking a cigarette. The smoke drifted into shapes that joined together. I knew how difficult it was to escape this kind of fog. Frost nipped at my dormant, repressed body; I enjoyed the cold. I was afraid of my own obsessions, and after a desperate attempt to get hold of my emotions, feverish desire escaped from within me. I was torn apart by a passion I could find no way to quell. My secrets buried in the dust began to plague me.

Within moments, I had gone back over my entire life. I don't own anything I have, or else I simply don't want it. Perhaps I don't know what I want, but I know that I don't want to be Sami's wife. I didn't choose the purse I carry every day—it was a gift from my mother. Wearing my hair pulled back made me feel that my femininity was extinct, or outdated. I chose the button-down shirts that filled my closets because they showed I was a respectable woman. This is what I wanted to be. But even the perfume I wore was a gift from one of my female relatives. Because I no longer cared how I smelled, I would spray any scent on my body.

My sister squawks nonstop chatter; the makeup kit that she bought me doesn't suit my skin tone, but I wear it every day anyway. It's strange how we hate small details about things when we aren't happy, but when we feel good and pleased with life, we're able to overcome them. I got my life back, but still felt that memory was cheating me. I had always clung onto life but had rarely truly lived. My world was filled with victims and executioners, with deliberate dreams that dissociated me from my soul. It's the image of my father, smoking a cigar in the corner of the house, reckoning with his disappointments and his desire to withdraw from the world. It's my mother counting the compensation money he received when he returned from Kuwait. And it's the sound of their only quarrel, which still reverberates in my head to this day, filling me with resentment. It makes me want tear myself apart when Sami beats me in front of the kids.

My way to escape reality from the time I was a child: to imagine other people and other lives until I could fall asleep. I don't know when I started having sexual fantasies, but they seem to have always been there. I don't know why I've always liked to have no control in my fantasies. I let imaginary people do what they want to my body and control it. Perhaps it was a hidden desire to search for safety, a place that would hold onto me, where I would be trapped, unable to resist, submissive and satisfied.

When I got a little older, I became more sophisticated in my fantasies. I was obsessed by the idea of not being a virgin and found out that my girlfriends shared my obsession. We had never had sex and never dared touch that thing pulsating between our thighs, but yet we all feared it would not be as it was supposed to be, sealed up tightly. We were afraid blood wouldn't flow on our wedding nights and we were afraid of that wet feeling we got without warning, as if our honor resided between our thighs. This was by far my greatest fear. I didn't know how to protect this honor from my fantasies and didn't know where all of my feelings of desire came from.

Now I don't know if I was afraid so much as I was impatient to explore and discover the taboo. I regret that no one ever taught me anything about my body. The culture of panic that was visible on the faces of everyone around me if so much as the word "kiss" was mentioned made me feel that I had encroached on a forbidden zone, which I was scared to enter but whose contours I desired to discover. Silent noise surrounded the topic of the body.

When summer arrived, with all its sticky humidity, I would make my way to the bathtub as if sneaking into a secret, remote cave. I would lie under the water, letting it combat the dry, fragrant heat.

Since childhood, the sun had been my companion as I scrambled down rough roads, climbed up boulders, and played in the dirt when we visited our relatives. I used to love watching my Auntie Samia climb up onto the roof of the house on a tall ladder leaning against the inside wall. My auntie was small and slim, her sallow oval face lined with pronounced wrinkles. Her delicate lips were purple and her face expressed pure kindness. She evoked a contradictory mixture of compassion and disgust in me. It was as if her eroding girlish youthfulness had bottomed out. She talked about her glory days, when she was blessed with thick, long, blonde braids. I wondered to myself why women criticize allure and beauty in public while privately they sing their own praises? Does this reveal a kind of surrender to a hidden femininity, one that, no matter how hard you try to bury it under values and chastity, still manages to resurface as if implicitly ordered by Eve herself?

Is this what I was doing? Did I deny my femininity because I learned from them how it dies before it is even born? How a woman is judged by what she conceals of herself? Is it because the intensity of the sun exhausted me that I found a bridge to my Self in the breeze on the balcony? Did Sami's humiliating beatings make my dignity whimper and my pride scream out from within my veins, telling me, "Revolt! Be who you want to be!"?

CHAPTER 19

I trained myself in infidelity, and it became like a profession, or a religion I had converted to. I contemplated my reflection in the mirror and teased my hair so it would look thicker. I flipped my head upside down quickly, so the style would look natural. I heard the sounds of an Egyptian film on TV coming from the other room and laughed. Whenever I was on a date with Rabih, I would laugh at the smallest thing. I became more flexible and more fun. Even though I was supposed to be afraid, hand trembling as I applied blusher to my cheeks, voice strangulated and vocal cords strained, I was happy instead.

I transformed into a hypocrite and a thief, stealing a few minutes of happiness. As my trysts with my lover approached, I treated my husband nicer, as a kind of revenge. I shunned him as my passion for the man I loved got stronger, as if to say, "This is the passion that has been forbidden to me. It manifests itself in sin to save me from routine and boredom." This monotony had spilled all down my body and Rabih licked it right off of me. I will be unfaithful to your boring life. All these lies you've told yourselves; I will be unfaithful to them. This honor you've said I must protect; I will be unfaithful to it.

I invented a tale and kept it in my mind. Through it, I saw the woman I was at home: destroyed, battered, constrained, and burnt out. I am a woman whose portrait hangs on the wall. The more you try to brush the dust off it, the more it sticks. I am a woman like my mother who tries to heal the rifts in her life but is in denial that life is rotten to the core.

I remember my father's long nights away from home at work, even before he started traveling abroad so often. My mother would put her Self aside and practice saying nice things, which came out lame and made no sense. She would often stay up reading until morning, in the hope that she could match the culture and knowledge of her extreme-leftist husband. But no matter how desperately she tried, she was unable to properly pronounce the name Ernesto Che Guevara. Neglecting us, she passed long evenings and nights sobbing into her pillow.

Anticipating my father's return, she would get up early in the morning and rush outside, because he rarely informed her when he would be back home. Often, he would come back very late and fall asleep on the living room sofa. She threw herself into her housework in the mornings to forget her thirsty loneliness. I imagined my mother in a prison that clipped women's wings and housed their breakdowns when no one praised them. Noting her clothes hanging lifeless in her closet, I asked myself, "Does my father love her? Does she love him? Is her steadfastness and vigor, which fluctuates between her silence and her attempts to keep up with his knowledge, the truth? Or is the truth actually a bitterness that is not yet fully bitter, buried deep within her body?"

Since my father always treated me kindly, I always blamed my mother for the harsh way he treated her. I thought that she must be the reason that he spent so much time away from home. I never knew that she was in a state of despair so deep that no one could reach her. Her severe external appearance concealed that she was clinging onto our family and a life that had forced her to deny her own sensitive, feminine side.

With time, my mother no longer waited for my father to come home from work. She stopped memorizing revolutionary ideologies or the definitions of things like imperialism. She started to enjoy going out and having visits with the neighbors. She no longer minded housework and busied herself with cooking and cleaning. She seemed to have embraced her inferiority to him, or maybe she secretly despised him. A man, no matter how cultured and knowledgeable, doesn't mean much to a woman if he doesn't provide her with warmth and protection.

She started regularly cursing Lenin and Stalin, holding them accountable for her misery. When the son of one of our neighbors married a Russian girl, she took the opportunity to stigmatize her, denouncing her with hateful epithets within the earshot of all the local women, "All we ever got from Russia were complexes. Have we run out of local girls to marry in our country?" My mother went on insulting the Communist Party and the Soviet Union, especially Che Guevara who "personally ruined" her life.

She kept on muttering these strange words, and the neighbors started to believe what she said about how loose foreign girls were. "Is that one who Azzam married really better than Imm Hassan's daughter? She's as good as gold!" She carried on pouring out her anger on the leftists, "Has it gotten so bad that we now need to marry Russian whores?"

That was the first time that I'd actually seen her break down in public. She locked herself up in her room that day, doing nothing but lying on the bed staring at the books piled up on my father's bookshelves, cursing the circumstances that forced her to leave school. She wanted to feel like a woman; she wanted her husband to buy her a fashionable dress, like her friend Imm Farid's husband did. But my arrogant father was immersed in his reading. He was stingy with love, and any expression of it outside of sex. Indeed, he denied her love, leaving her stuck with three children and permanently unfulfilled desires.

I was just about to go out when I heard the sound of the TV. I felt that I was leaving my husband as I made my way through the winding alleys. I hoped he wouldn't be there when I returned, that he had realized I wasn't right for him and found another woman and forsaken me. He would reject me, and I would be rid of him.

He chewed his food and watched the movie. I kissed him on both cheeks spitefully, like someone paying the price for a crime they are about to commit in advance. He thought I was going to meet Hala and go with her to a doctor's appointment for her son's diabetes. He said, "I wish you'd go out with Hala every day. You kiss me without me having to ask!" I laughed and slipped out joyfully, only a few steps away from my lover's apartment and my secret life.

I knew it was no longer possible to go back to being that dreamy young woman who hid her Self like she hid forbidden letters that came in the post. I had to admit something else to myself too: that I loved men, that is to say, masculine beings. Men were the ferocity that I was lacking and needed to be complete. In my fantasies, I searched for their sensitive, aesthetic side, which was exotic, rare, and cut off from them.

At the beginning of my relationship with my husband, I

foolishly sought to minimize all that unjustified power that he had and turn his dark, troubled being into a kind man. When he always ended up apologizing and crying after beating me, I found myself stuck, mumbling my thoughts, as if they were small pieces of ideas stifled in a cage. I felt obligated to forgive him. Was I forgiving him because I was a mother and this meant I had to be synonymous with idealized perfection, always the model of superior morals, free of any anger or remonstrance? I remained an ideal being within my surroundings and crushed within my Self.

When he hit me, I was unable to stand up to him; I was that Self, withdrawn for fear of this angry man's delusional authority. He bored deep into the inner curves and tunnels of my body to satisfy lusts and desires he had long suppressed. I absorbed all the blows that Sami meted out upon me, knowing my blood would be shed here and feeling that I deserved the punishment. I knew I had to be strong enough to withstand the pain he would inflict on me.

When I was isolated and all alone, I felt like a person newly emerging from a miserable period of wandering amongst the enemy. Nothing was left of me but dust. God had cursed me with desire and a love of life. My imagination protected me from everything, but I was like an old wooden box with bits of dresses stored in it. How can Sahar ever forgive me for all the humiliation I inflicted upon her when in my dreams I was the one who promised to show her beauty and truth?

He wanted to completely undo me, to rub my face in fear. He was exactly like the people in the neighborhood who wanted to shun my father, or Shaykh Bilal, who wanted to control my mother's mind, or the shaykhs at the Mansouri Great Mosque who wanted to exclude anyone who dared question their perfection.

He did succeed in keeping me from my Self in a certain way. I knew from my attempts to sketch some interior designs how depressed I'd become. I ended up drawing a tablecloth sliding down off its table into a bottomless pit. I was no longer able to use sparkly or bright colors, and I wound up with only dark, wooden shades. When I had finished drawing, I knew everything was difficult. I was like a woman vomiting up all the evil inside her.

Despite all this, my old habits of interacting with my Self converged. I clung to strange fantasies and delusions. I could no longer deny that my relationship with Rabih had unexpectedly refined my personality. The sex we had together was an example of the very art of giving up control over the other person, removing the cloud of fear that had wounded my soul. I must admit that my distance from the sacred and my proximity to heathen impurity was the only way to find a common point between them.

After meeting Rabih, I started buying sexy lingerie and all those pretty accessories I'd never bought before. He was an especially sensitive man who loved details. As he ran his fingers along my body, I became another woman—not from this universe. I was his woman, and his alone. The scent of my body changed and burst forward in passion from the very tips of my hair.

He used to enter me panting, until his body seemed like it was floating in the air above mine. I gave myself to him and dug my nails into his back. I wanted him deeper and deeper inside me so I could keep him there. When that sticky liquid squirted out onto my breasts and stomach, it flowed out with love. We stopped talking. I could almost hear my past life weeping in those sounds of silence. I embraced his body; it had become a part of me. But it wasn't actually merely a part of me. Rabih was all of me. He was my entire being, the pure nectar of existence that I sip from.

The very few times I fell asleep next to him, we stuck right together after having reached mutual orgasms. I sometimes used to wait for him to fall asleep next to me, and then lay my chest atop his, with my vulva on his stomach. I could then hear his breathing, which remained feverish, as if he were still having sex with me without being aware of it.

CHAPTER 20

With a hemorrhaging memory, I felt like my mind was dancing. I remember the day my father caught me sitting on the edge of the pool with my friend Sawsan's brother. He lost his mind. He turned into an angry predator and forbade me from visiting the village for several months. Me speaking to a man was a crime, and me being of the other gender reflected back to my father that I should never be left alone.

If things had been normal in my family, I wouldn't give all these details such exaggerated importance. But, like my extended family, they were obsessed with details that weren't all that important. How could a liberal, leftist man transform into a fearful, raging beast determined to keep his daughter away from sin? What culture made him treat me like a helpless child who couldn't look after herself? Was his rejection of my mother a rejection of desires and therefore a prohibition on himself that he projected into a prohibition on me?

Perhaps after seeing the enormity of the situation, I became more understanding of my father. I wanted to protect him from rejection and isolation. I understood why he was afraid for me, because he understood that we were forbidden from dreaming and living life. He chose a living death, because the other death would come sooner or later anyway.

He knew that walls collapse, plans fail, sorrows prey on living beings, evil triumphs, friends die, and parents will see the blood of their children if they send them abroad. He knew that self-betrayal might turn into a way of life. He knew that pictures lie, and that victory is not destiny and is indeed forbidden for our dark city, addicted to depression.

His atheism was perhaps partly inherited from values stipulating that whoever does not know the god chosen by the people of Medina, knows no other god, only Satan's messenger. Having already judged our grim future, my father found himself hostage to the fear of fear, a prisoner of his own disappointment. He never told me that mistakes are simply a part of life. Over and over again, he made me feel that time stops with our first failure, and that we should be humbled by this.

My mother also avoided speaking to me. A giant chasm opened up between us. My tension with her was different from her relationship with my siblings. My father spoiled me. I was his favorite, and this made her both jealous and also afraid of being touched by evil. She acted as though I were his alone. Since she had sworn to cut off any womanly feelings she had for him completely, she was stingy in how she treated me, replacing mothering with coldness and an excess of caution. I realized the full extent of this when I became a woman—the first time I got my period. That day, I went into the bathroom and noticed I had red spots in my underpants. Believing that it was normal, I simply changed my panties.

But when I went back in later, new drops of vivid bright red appeared on the toilet paper. My legs started shaking as if a fire were escaping from inside me. I called out to my mother. The tears clouding my eyes collided with the thin smile drawn on my mother's face. She handed me a sanitary towel and showed me how to stick it onto my underpants. She said, "My God, you've grown up Sahar, and now you've become a young lady." She let me know that it would be like this for a few days and that all girls bleed like this once a month, as they grow up. She told me it was normal and no reason to be afraid.

I didn't sleep at all that night. Something mysterious overtook my body. It wasn't an ache or a pain. Something I didn't understand was turning me into a woman. I became confused as strange sensations filled my body. The only thing I knew was that blood was flowing out from between my thighs and was being soaked up by the sanitary pad, which my mother had shown me how to attach correctly.

My father didn't agree to let us visit the village again until I'd assured him that I wouldn't go out without his permission. I swore I wouldn't speak to Sawsan if we ran into her. We piled into the car and I gazed out the window at the road stretching from the coast up to my village perched on the hillside. My father stopped and bought my siblings and me chocolate bars and Pepsi. He paid for them, we got back into the car, and off we flew. During the journey, I kept thinking of how I could meet up with Sawsan's brother without my father knowing about it. I tried to push this out of my mind, but the more I tried, the more the idea of meeting him dominated my thoughts.

As usual, I went to visit my father's sister Samia when we first arrived. That's where I was when I spotted Sawsan's brother from a distance. I hurried away in the opposite direction, my body skidding over the roadside, and kept going until finally I stopped and turned. He was staring at me, surprised and disappointed. He waved at me and beckoned me to me to come closer, but my fear was stronger than I was. I was terrified of disobeying my father and for him to stop loving me. I ran far away from the boy who I really wanted to go out with. My desire stumbled along the road, sweat dripping off it, and I ran off, swift as the wind. I couldn't help but think that I was fighting the air, that I was engaged in a battle on all sides. I kept running and sobbing, my feet keeping time with my pounding heart, with the heat and passion I wanted to surrender myself to. Running away is really just the flip side of desire. I ran so far from what I wanted out of fear, indeed from denial of what I wanted from life. I started searching for what I was supposed to want. My father's admonitions lived within me, my mother's misfortune rained down upon me, along with my Auntie Samia's repressed desires: How was I supposed to cope with the overwhelming number of people inside of me?

When I got to Aunt Samia's house, tears were running down my cheeks and I was dripping with sweat. Fear laid my heart bare, as if I were about to die. I buried myself in her embrace and asked her to hold me tight. My eyes were clouded. My gaze was confused. I was shaken by a squeezing pain. My aunt comforted me and asked me what was wrong. I told her that something was happening in my body and I couldn't talk to anyone about it. I explained what had happened in the bathroom and what my mother said. Then I told her about my meetup with Sawsan's brother near the pond. I carried on talking about how I was afraid that no one would marry me now that I was no longer a good girl, how just having this one conversation with a boy had made so much blood flow out of me. My aunt laughed out loud, and as the sound filled the space, my indignation grew.

She sat me down and brought me a glass of my favorite drink, sweet mulberry juice. She started telling me about when her mother had begun experiencing episodes of memory loss so severe that she couldn't even remember her own children's names. She said she used to feel lonely in her family, that when she was younger she thought that her mother had forgotten her, didn't care about her, or purposely ignored her. She didn't realize that her mother was actually sick until she herself was older and started to understand what Alzheimer's was. She told me how much she suffered each time her mother's illness worsened, when she was able to understand her better.

"People think that children don't understand anything, but they're wrong," my aunt explained. "If you take them out of all the stress surrounding them, children realize things right in their core."

She assured me that I would understand my parents' behavior better when I got older, and that there would be an explanation for it. She told me not to panic, because it wasn't worth it. She explained things about the world of women to me, how our physiology is different from that of men. She told me that when little girls grow up, the blood that flows from them is a sign that they are maturing normally. There is no need for fear. Despite my aunt's attempts to simplify things and reassure me, I could still feel my insides being torn apart. I was a prisoner to an anxiety that kept ripping me up—a prisoner of running away as much as to what I was running away from.

When I married Sami, I fled from my parents. I felt that I had to find another kind of belonging—to people unlike them.

I like someone who emigrates because they are weary of their homeland. I was a suitcase, a body in transit, searching for an identity unlike that of the women I knew. My total absorption in Sami's limited world at the beginning of our relationship was a kind of recognition that I belonged to him. The world of my parents had less space inside me and gave way to his world. But in this world that I considered soft and gentle, another man was oppressing me. The specters of his family, and the feeling that they were swirling all around me whenever he hit me, controlled me. I fled from Sami to Rabih. Would I flee Rabih one day? What is this need within me to get away? Was it really a desire to escape my Self? Or a journey to find it?

CHAPTER 21

Behind their metal gates, the gods roll the dice. It's as if we slip through their fingers and find ourselves alive on earth. Rabih was born in a tiny ground floor apartment, not even forty square meters in size. Its inhabitants' heads nearly touched the ceiling. His parents slept on a fold-out sofa that filled the entire room. Every morning they would fold it back up, while Rabih and his siblings would pack up the mattresses spread on the remaining floor space and hide them in a corner along with the sheets and pillows.

Even before his father's early retirement, Rabih had to work after school, and his dreams of being a pilot, traveling from one country to another, dissipated. His dreams felt as useless as the miserable, impoverished land that created him. The features of his father, a simple vegetable seller, accompanied him in all the winding alleys he passed through as he delivered his goods to merchants and shopkeepers.

He was like a peddler, carrying thousands of things each day for people he didn't know. No one ever carried anything for him. Rabih had a very sensitive stomach. He was often greatly affected by the cold, which seeped into the bones of his weak body. His mother would wait for him with a cup of hot black tea to warm up his joints. Rabih didn't play outside in the courtyards like the other boys. And he had to wear his torn shoes and clothes with holes until he outgrew them.

His classmates made fun of his threadbare school bag, pointing at him and calling him, "peddler." But the little boy who drew his strength from nothingness got the better of them—not only in schoolwork, but also by selling them candies and chocolates for a cheaper price than they'd been paying. Little by little, Rabih came to be admired by all of his classmates.

As he grew older, he changed his business. In his teenage years, Rabih started supplying his classmates with porno films and Marlboro cigarettes. He didn't sell the cigarettes by the pack, but individually to make more money. Individual cigarettes brought maximum profits. Learning didn't mean much any more to this boy, who'd become a "little earner." School for him had become a shopping mall where he was able to earn an income to supplement what he made from peddling in the afternoons.

However, the material wealth flowing through his fingers did not satisfy this boy whose childhood had been cut short. He wanted his friends to like him for who he was, complete with wounds and pride, not simply as a petty merchant who could fill their orders. He wanted to run around on the playing fields with them instead of always being a spectator at their matches, watching from afar. He wanted one of them to give him things, instead of always waiting for him to give them things.

Feelings of loneliness, isolation, and lack of love made him thirsty for shared emotional connection. He never reached the point of being cruel, despite his hardened appearance and ungrateful gaze, which covered up the confused, terrified child he was. Rabih knew the very worst kind of fear, the kind of fear that cloaks a person without his ever realizing it, the fear of hitting rock bottom. Rabih's exhaustion imprinted itself on his very features; traces of pain showed on his forehead and his feet.

He was always anxious. There was always a glint of torture in his eyes. He kept his anger and sense of aggrievement at the world hidden and rarely spoke of his sorrow. I remember the day he told me about his mother's passing. He described the melancholy feeling of returning to their old house and not finding her. I still think about something he once said to me: "We even miss sadness when it's gone, Sahar." Do you really miss sorrow? Do we get so used to suffering that we can't break free of it?

"My mother no longer hummed the tunes she'd memorized. Even the smell of the house changed after she passed, Sahar. Death has its own scent. Food didn't have the same taste. No one looked at me the way she used to," Rabih would say.

He hardly ever mentioned his father, who'd passed away that same year, except to note his kind, exhausted eyes. Neither of them could bear to live without the other's misery. Rabih then found himself responsible for two children, except he'd never even had sex with a woman or procreated. They were just there. He stumbled through his childhood, adolescence, and young adulthood, and then life overtook him before he could reach a handout for help. He turned into a strong, solid man who performed all of his tasks quickly and skillfully.

He therefore chose Hanadi to be his wife. She was a simple, quiet girl who was able to help with the difficulties of his daily life while he was getting himself established. Little by little, dust turned to gold in the hands of that young man whose life had gone off the rails.

Rabih saved his money and opened a shop where he sold everything from videocassettes to CDs to underwear to sneakers. The store carried items he could purchase at a very low price and then resell at a small profit. Slowly his business grew, and he started traveling abroad to bring in imported goods.

I have always wondered if the source of Rabih's money was sheer effort, or if he had to give up what we would call principles on his way to a quick profit in order to belong. Turning a profit became an unquenchable desire because money gave him social value. Previously he'd had practically no social status, and experienced the contempt that people have for the lives and disappointments of the poor.

He often walked with his head bowed, eyes to the ground, praying for relief from insults and oppression—like a lover without his beloved, forbidden, secret and fugitive dreams. He wanted to replace his patched-up sports jacket and old-fashioned shoes with fancy new ones, no matter the cost. He was willing to sacrifice his own humanity in favor of that of society, which had no mercy, compassion, or place for anything but power and money. This is what his life experience had taught him.

He became so used to this that he even forgot that his truncated childhood had been lurking in the corners of his regular life. He never forgot that no one liked him when he'd been an impoverished peddler in desperate need of love. He would never know if the friends who gathered around him now would have done the same if he hadn't managed to change his life situation. The doubts and trauma folded into his memories haunted him, but he stood tall, victorious over his pain. Behind his haughty demeanor lay a brokenness, that of a boy who had to become a man before his time.

Because we are so often attracted to those people who share our pain, I felt responsible for making him feel less sad. I wanted him to know that there are other emotions that one can feel in life—including those that have nothing to do with what we have achieved, what we own, and that these are worth more than the sadness embedded within him. My feelings transformed into a kind of obsession with saving him from the clutches of capitalism. I wanted to somehow prove that the socialist thought that my father believed in was true. Isn't this what we do when we aren't able to save ourselves? We reflect our desires onto a mirror called the Other and we love it so much we hope it erases all the cruelty in our own minds. What about the duality of rejection and acceptance in my father's approach? Had this father of mine become a part of me, despite me rejecting him? Was I deep down rejecting Sami's approach and his surroundings?

I was also caught between the two currents of Sami's and my father's worlds. I tried to find a safe island somewhere between them, somewhere that I related to. Or even to find another man I related to. Was it lust or affection that linked me to my lover? Or was it a desire to satisfy my libido, which I refused to acknowledge except in my fantasies? When it materialized, I was captive to it, unable to be satiated by anything else.

What was I to him? A lifeline. A dream that mitigates the weight of the truth. A woman who can bring him what he wants but who he can't allow to pass through the buffer of his marital responsibilities and quick profits. A woman who will receive him but won't ever take him or overstep the real distance inherent in the relationship, for fear of destroying it altogether. When we follow love for its luster and beauty, we forget the dark clouds that can appear later. Our inability to contain the Other can become a tragedy whose orbit we are drawn into, like a prisoner circling a narrow cell when the door is actually open because they know no other world. The unknown is always open to everchanging possibilities.

Rabih was in a constant race against time. He was plagued by feelings that he had to accomplish everything quickly. He lived by rote, his life a machine in constant motion. He didn't enjoy anything he had. He was happy with everyone around him: his simple wife, Hanadi, who wanted to transform into a high-society woman and whose features started to become those of the wife of an important man; his two brothers who treated him like he was a winning lottery ticket, there to provide them with endless money; and his friends who sought refuge in him in times of trouble.

Rabih lost his sense of being alive. He got used to making love to his wife quickly to get it over with. She didn't understand much about affairs of the body. He lost the feeling of sexual pleasure with her. When he tried to have sex with Hanadi in the positions he'd seen in the porno films he'd sold as a child, she begged him to just be satisfied with their usual sex.

Hanadi had never seen a penis other than her husband's. What's more, when she saw it for the first time, she nearly vomited. She was afraid and started crying. Rabih convinced her to let him enter her, but he failed to arouse her whatsoever. In her mind, lust was forbidden and shameful, even in relations with her husband. Hanadi was born in a poor neighborhood to a modest, religious family. Her strict father and conservative mother could not understand the notion of a daughter having lustful feelings.

She had a husband in order to make babies and to take care of him. For her this meant preparing his food, ironing his clothes, washing and polishing his floors. She didn't care about his personal affairs; her job was to take care of the domestic sphere. She had no image in her mind of what it meant to be man and woman, male and female, or husband and wife. For her, marriage simply meant duties: food, drink, and household expenses.

As her husband's material situation improved, she became aware of new spheres in life. She started buying clothes with a fresh, clean scent, after so many years of her skin being rubbed raw by the harsh woolen shirts that she and her siblings had passed between each other. They settled on her skin and misery gnawed away at her. With her change of clothes, her spirit changed as well. She was no longer a grubby little girl, features shaped by poverty etched in the lines on her face. She had become a woman and she wanted to be like the women she saw on television. She didn't desire simply to look seductive and beautiful, but to feel that she was clean and had value—that she could bring in a Sri Lankan maid to serve her if she wanted.

She started going to the beauty salon to get manicures and remove her body hair. Hanadi fell in love with herself. She adored taking bubble baths and spent hours soaking luxuriously. She also liked going to the cinema. She left the theater crying every time she went, even if the film she'd watched wasn't particularly emotional. Whenever her girlfriends asked her why she was crying, she would claim that one scene or another had affected her. But she was lying. She cried because when she went to the cinema, she remembered the poverty that had previously prevented her from entering such an "elegant place," as she used to think of it. She cried because she'd never eaten popcorn as a girl, she only rarely had been able to watch television, and had never had a Barbie or a doll whose hair she could brush and clothes she could change. She would cry as she wondered, "Does getting things late and at the wrong time make up for not getting things?"

As Hanadi was retrieving the strands of her life from distant memories, she also feared losing the luxury to which she had become accustomed. Beautiful things were meant to carry on forever, but films always come to an end. She drank a glass of lemonade and realized as she sipped it how much she'd begun to love deliciousness.

She started to sink her teeth into pleasure and joyful moments. She played with her children. She bought coloring books for herself as well as for them. Despite her newfound elegance, she remained both a little girl and a teenager trapped in a grown woman's body. All the while, her existence with Rabih remained her only image of married life. She wasn't looking for love. She sought out joy, and this had nothing to do with a man. She was happy to transform their home into a doll's house. Dolls have no lustful feelings. Hanadi's lust remained buried deep inside her. Rabih kept searching for a woman.

He found out about Madame Nahla's chalet at the Azure private beach club and started going there once or twice a week. He went in search of women who would act like the porn stars he saw in films; they'd touch his penis and give him blow jobs. He had a burning desire to enjoy sex in this underworld, to watch himself come on the bodies of prostitutes. Like him, they were tainted by the poverty of their pasts and the search for wealth. He started to enjoy quick pleasure and cheap bodies. Like him, this pleasure had no value. Despite his disgust and revulsion, he was addicted to them because they reflected this dark part of himself. Few of his friends, dazzled by his new wealth, knew about this side of him.

As a client, Madame Nahla found him to be a catch, as he showered money on her. She reserved the most beautiful girls for him. She never knew if he preferred fair girls or dark girls. When she asked him, he told her he didn't have a preference. Rabih didn't care about these kinds of details in a woman. He didn't spend a long time gazing at the woman he was having sex with. He had few words, only commands. All he cared about was getting off, nothing more. He wasn't searching for emotions. He was convinced that the women he had sex with were not at all like his innocent child-wife. It would be impossible for his wife to be a prostitute because she had no lust or desire at all and was terrified to look at his penis.

His wife was a revised version of his mother. The women he had sex with at Madame Nahla's chalet were rude and shameless; they tried to seduce him so he would pay more. They wore scandalous clothes and bright red lipstick and trailed the scent of cheap, imitation perfumes. His wife wore only French perfume. His wife was innocent, and they were prostitutes. If he ever began to feel empathy for any one of them, he immediately cut it off. He knew that they were like him—excluded from life. Thus, he hated them and acted extremely arrogant toward them. It was as if he were retaliating against them for his own poverty. He would steal a bit of pleasure, and get off, watching his own sticky liquid smeared on their bodies.

CHAPTER 22

Dunya stood in the corner of the room, listening to her father berate me. Tareq held her hand and his eyelids held back a tear. Sami was holding me by the hair and pulling me back. My face was contorted upward and my body bent over backward in a degrading position.

I shouted at him, "Shame on you, in front of the children. We need to be rid of you, get off me!" As soon as the words were out of my mouth, he began slapping me, beating me, and taunting me. My body fell to the ground, and I could no longer hear anything but the wails of my children reverberating in my soul. Sami stopped and the children rushed into the living room in a panic. He turned on the TV and told them to sit down. They didn't dare move. I stayed on the ground—that's where I belonged, waiting for more of his blows to rain down on me. I no longer suffered any physical pain and my desire to fight back had ended. I wanted to die. I wished he would just kill me and put an end to this torture. Whenever I reached rock bottom like this, my self worth crumbled, as did my humanity. I became simply something for Sami to smash and trample under his feet.

All manner of contradictory thoughts swam through my mind: Am I such a nobody? Why did God create me? What should I do? With whom should I take refuge? Am I guilty? But he didn't even know that I had been unfaithful to him. He beat me long before I ever cheated on him.

I tried to get up, but I couldn't. Something was pulling me to the ground. It wasn't just that I was weak. I couldn't feel my hands, my feet, my eyes, or even my nose. I couldn't move my fingers; I was unable to breathe. I wept deep inside myself, calling on everything I knew from the religiosity of the people in my neighborhood and the culture of my father, wins and losses, my unfulfilled dreams. The thin protection I had wrapped around myself peeled away. Motionless, on the ground where there was nothing but depravity and bitterness, I wondered, "How did God create people? Are humans predators?" There are no predators in the books my father sought refuge in, nor are there any in our empty house that he tried to prevent any Others from entering.

I dared not look into my children's eyes—a powerful regret for bringing them into this world would overtake me. Sami approached me and held out his hand to help me stand up. I looked at his dilated pupils. His face had turned into a sheet of ice, whose coldness I couldn't escape. It was ready to surge at me. My hand reached out to him on its own. Everything inside of me was beckoning to me to not go with him, but my body parts all acted as if they belonged to him. He sat me down on the edge of the bed and started apologizing for what he'd done. He went on to make excuses that I didn't listen to. I was unconscious like a tamed, trained circus animal. Instead of commanding me to run or jump, my husband would order me to open my thighs and let him come inside me. Sami violated me and I suffocated when his fingers touched my breasts. Less than an hour earlier this man had been beating me, and now he was having sex with me. I felt like I was in one of those crumbling, abandoned villages where women walk hunched over, walking through dark cellars and windy labyrinths with no exit. I do not know.

Sami finished. I got up and went in to check on the children. They rushed onto my lap. I patted their heads and tried to justify what happened by saying their father had been angry. I asked them to forget what had just happened and promised them that everything would be fine. Sami came in and stood at a distance. They looked at him in terror. I tried to just power through this appalling situation and put them to bed. I pretended to doze off in Dunya's bed and waited for him to fall asleep.

In my mind, I pictured Rabih, lying with his wife or playing with his children. I drew a picture-perfect image of the ideal family for him with his wife and kids. I saw myself in one of those villages where men beat their wives, where women are birds with clipped wings. I kept expelling this image from my mind only for it to reappear. I fell asleep and woke with this image singed on my flesh and skin, as if the remnants of these imaginary villages ran through my blood. I was exiled in my own house, in my own big and small homeland. What is this justice people talk about? Does justice shed tears? Does justice weep?

After I lost contact with my Self—that is to say with my imagination, which began innocently in my childhood and expanded with time to take on intensely erotic forms—I no longer knew who I was. If I looked forward, I went involuntarily backward. I was a person stuck in a bleak moment, sapped of my strength because I didn't believe in it. Sami convinced me that he needed to beat me, Rabih that I was destined to be his lover. Humiliation doesn't even evoke indignation in me sometimes. Instead it makes me feel that we are leftovers and don't deserve to exist. Am I the liberated woman, lover of Rabih, or the woman enslaved by Sami? Is it my freedom to sneak into an apartment or a beach chalet and express my Self, my love, my existence—paralyzed by fear, if only for a few hours?

In the moment, feelings of pity for that Self haunted me and began to mount up inside. I floated within these walls, drowning in these thoughts. My realization that this connection with my Self was impossible and transformed into holding onto an Other as something that was possible. The Other woman calmly approached me: naked, beautiful, luminous. She started taking off my clothes, stroking my face, and brushing strands of my hair out of my eyes. She kissed me tenderly on the forehead. She held my hand and passed it over my body, telling me that I was beautiful. I told her, "I wish I were you." She stood right in front of me. She gathered me into her arms and joined her body to mine. She got under my skin. Our hair became one, our blood became one, our spirit became one.

I went to Rabih's apartment the next day, the signs of the beating concealed by my clothing. He stood there staring at me. My fingers trembled, my breathing was uneven, and I looked at him like a fugitive with no place left to hide. He held me tight and I cried on his chest like a little girl. I didn't just cry. I was wracked with sobs. Between breaths, a voice shouted out from deep inside me. He brought me a glass of water, balancing it against my lips. I sipped from it and he waited for me to calm down a little. I remained stunned into silence. My tears confused me. He brushed away the strands of my hair that had fallen over my forehead and held my face between his hands, pressing against it to express his anger. I asked him to stop and he refused. I asked him why he was pushing so hard against my forehead, and he said that it pained him to see me like this, when he was so powerless to help me.

His fingers invaded my forehead. He started rubbing my face, his fingers passing over my eyes and forehead and touching my eyelids. I kissed the palm of his hand and my tears dampened his fingertips. I threw myself onto his lap so I could absorb some of his gentle kindness. I started slowly to melt into him. I swore to myself I would sleep with him with the same vigor that my husband had beat me. I rested my head on his left shoulder and asked him if he loved me. He replied, "Of course I love you; do you doubt that?" I asked him what it meant that we loved each other, and why we couldn't be together. He answered, "You're married, Sahar, have you forgotten?" I wanted to answer, "You're married too," but I didn't say anything. I realized that this was the first time that I couldn't say what I was thinking, not even to Rabih, for fear that he wouldn't understand. I closed my eyes and chose to think of nothing but the pleasure I would experience, and the secret revenge I was taking on Sami, his insults, and my mother's coldness. This pleasure was a statement that we women have libidos too.

I took off the features of the depressed woman and put on the courage that good sex had taught me. I took his hand and started stroking his palm with my fingers. I untied my hair and let it hang down over my shoulders. Rabih wanted to speak. I indicated that he should keep silent. He kept staring at my hand. He leaned over me, his lips moistened my neck, and his tongue tickled my earlobes. I closed my eyes and moaned softly.

Whenever he heard my voice, he kissed me more. He moved to my breasts and began biting my nipples like a baby. I dug my fingernails into his back, hugged him tightly, and kissed his lower belly until taking his penis into my mouth. He touched my vulva at the same time. I was dripping wet. He turned me over onto my back and we held hands as he entered me. He was inside of me and we became one, just as happened when the woman in the shadows and I became one. I wanted him to capture that excess passion and I wanted him to understand how much I desperately needed him.

When he reached his orgasm, I asked him to stay inside of me. My eyes were taking in the details of the room—the wooden wardrobe in the corner, the round white table next to the sofa, laden with magazines and a worn tablecloth that resembled his traditional sofa. There were no paintings on the wall. It was the first time I'd noticed that Rabih's apartment had nothing but the basics in earth-toned colors.

He got up to bring me coffee. I sat up in bed, looking at the window and the curtains covering it, my chin leaning on my knee, thinking about what my life might look like in five years or so. I didn't feel safe, so it was only natural that these kinds of questions might pass through my mind. I thought about what would happen if there were to be a change in who I was. I wandered through my dark, repetitive days with black-and-blue marks covering my body. I thought about how I was cheating on Sami and wanted to be free of him. Rabih came up behind me and kissed my head. I turned toward him and moved over so he could sit next to me. He put his arms around my waist and pulled me toward him. I looked at him and said, "Do you see that closed window covered by a curtain? One day I am going to open it and let myself go out and live life." He held onto my hair and said, "Let your hair hang down your back." I laughed and kissed his forehead, feeling much less anxious than when I'd arrived, and I left his apartment with more self-confidence.

Rabih was the only source I derived power from. His flat was the place where I could be myself. After I met him, I started looking in the mirror and reconciling with my body. I learned to love my shadow and my soul. After my trysts with him I became more able to give my children the love and affection they needed. I was better able to endure life when I was thinking about him. I'd grow impatient when there were long stretches between our meetings.

I left his apartment satiated and full of pleasure. But fear of this feeling ending might muddy my pure mood. I should bring a box to store up all the passion present in Rabih's apartment, so I could use it at home when he wasn't there. I wished that love could be a liquid that we could store in bottles and spray on ourselves every day like perfume, or that we could take it like a medicine to keep away diseases, psychological complexes, and emotional deprivation.

I pushed those feelings down, checked that my clothes were neat, and then got in the car. I turned up the radio and lowered the window so I could feel the air rushing against me. I felt that I was beautiful, younger, and transparent. My throat was tight and my breaths shallow and far apart. I lifted my head up to verify if there were any traces of kisses on my neck and found none.

I was happy because Sami's mother was going into hospital to undergo a medical procedure and he had to stay with her. I would have enough time to satisfy my desires and enjoy a little freedom. I used the children as an excuse to avoid visiting her, urging him to take care of her and not leave her alone during the day. I passed by the nearby bakery to buy sweets for the children, and I called Hala to tell her to meet me at my place. I entered my house to the sound of quiet music playing. I sat with Dunya and Tareq and we worked together on a coloring book. I felt absolute relief with Sami not there. My anxiety disappeared, replaced by joy, even in my imagination. I would imagine it in a physical form, sly smiling at me in an unspoken agreement to keep my secret.

Sami always stuck close to me, extremely jealously, and refused to give me any way to express my Self. He was like Tripoli, a city which had closed its ancient gates and expelled the Other from the folds of its memory to keep its inhabitants from knowing that there was a world outside it. If they saw this different world, they might stop pouring into the Mansouri mosque and they might become freer, or even communists like my father.

Every day, Tripoli seemed to grow more and more attached to its Islamic identity. There was a rise in strict, religious movements, waves of halal and haram, and it defended this emerging entity by rejecting or imprisoning the Other. I was exactly like a city—a woman with buried treasures within me, upon whose soil, buildings, and ruins dust had accumulated. Dirt had settled on its flags, just as the ugly marks of beatings showed on my body.

We were both so preoccupied with pain and destruction that we didn't notice the small opening for light to come in through the beards and corruption of the greedy and the capitalist political class that gave cover to the fundamentalist movements, condemning its miserable inhabitants to poverty.

When I looked at the abandoned part of any development in the city, closer to where my mother's side of the family lives, I imagined that the big buildings masked the narrowness of the roads. The silence around this emaciation and inequality was their right, because my relatives didn't need to air their dirty laundry to the outside world, just as I didn't need to spread the scandal of my husband's violence toward me. That's when I'd turn into a "fucking bitch" who'd bring the wrath of masculine power upon myself. It's most likely that no one would support me or take on the responsibility of defending me, just as no one would stand up for the people of Tripoli if they voiced their forbidden dreams. They would find no leaders to ease the collective rumbling of their empty bellies. Instead, they would be relegated to a circle of unbelievers, people outside the religious cliques and political factions.

It seemed to me that my very existence—the sense of distress and concern that was always with me in my being and nothingness—was related to my city and its absence from our country's map. What I mean is a lack of recognition of its effectiveness, its capacity to be more than a mere insignificant formality. Its dubious attachment to formal, visible, non-substantive religiosity was an age-old question for which I could find no specific answer.

Did this place where I was born really even exist compared with the capital city, or other more developed cities? Why did I always see the face of death in the groups of people leaving the Mansouri mosque? How could I see their dispersion when the worshipers all walked in one direction? I loved them when they were something forbidden to me as I spied on them from the window of my grandfather's house, but I started to hate them when I became a part of them, when I was woven into the fabric of their lives, a part of Sami's family.

Did I have to resemble the Other in order to belong, to be like my mother, my husband, my city, my father and his books? Did I have to join the textile weavers, the religious men, political parties, the village women? Did I have to be a part of everything and never ever reach that inner being that itself was Me? Is it absolutely necessary to be accepted by Others? Is worth the exorbitant price that we are paying? Must we prove that the choices of the Other are incorrect and feel superior in cultivating an illusion that we then call truth or custom? What right do we have to claim that knowledge is fixed and stable if we've hardly seen anything on this earth yet? Is it the fear of the unknown and the Other who is different that makes these people rush to promote their religion, their merchandise, their beliefs, their people, their gender, their dishwasher powder? Everything around us is subject to change, but we are stuck in what we claim to be absolutely right out of fear of this change and life's surprises. We push away what we do and don't want at the same time.

I don't know if my infidelity reflected this nothingness, or this great true love, or this ideal image of a relationship that I was reaching for. I did realize one thing though. A secret strength had started to move inside me, pushing me toward being, with all of the hardships, questions, obsessions, dreams, fantasies, hopes, and suffering that the journey carried with it.

Sami was my jailer and executioner for more than ten years, during which he kept me operating within his logic. He stripped me down to a false identity that I never once felt truly existed. I remember how he used to come with me to buy clothes, offering his opinions on how I looked and purposely embarrassing me in front of the shopkeepers. I was compelled to remain silent, to swallow my humiliation in front of strangers and his friends, because I knew that if I spoke or aroused his anger in any way, he wouldn't hesitate to beat me or publicly berate me.

When I began objecting to things inside the house, he turned from a man who claimed to love me into a monster who would abuse me. I was his doll, as he used to always repeat. I was that Barbie doll whose hand he would break off and then stick it back on again. I was a doll who he put on display and took great pleasure looking at. Dolls endure the irritation and wrath of the children who play with them. They play with their dolls when they want to and then toss them aside whenever they feel like it. He scribbled in the notebook of my life; his pale pencil pierced me, devoured my throat, and laughed at how broken I was.

The strange thing is that after he beat me, in a matter of moments he would be drowning in a river of tears, as if he were a spoiled little boy, drooling and weeping in front of a shop window, wanting to devour the world and everything in it. He buried his head in my chest and pulled my arms around him telling me I was his mother, whose love and care he cannot live without. So I'd changed from a doll into his mother, and then suddenly into a whore. Now I can see how I used to contemplate his emotions and absorb them. I changed to play the roles he chose, I imitated and mastered them even if grudgingly. No, I wasn't simply imitating them, I became them and they possessed me. I sometimes really felt pity for him, and cared for him with a mother's tenderness. Or I acted like his doll who would respond to all of his wishes and desires. Did I start cheating on him to prove to him that I could be a whore as he accused me of being? I snapped out of the annoying thoughts that had started to follow me around all of the corridors of the house, as if they emanated out through the wooden doors or seeped through the ivory paint on the walls. I heard a light knock on the door. Hala entered, proclaiming loudly in English, "Hell, you are glowing!"

She winked at me, indicating that she knew I had just made love with Rabih. She opened her arms and I gave her a big hug. She showered me with praise, commending my beauty: "Love does miracles, no?" She then started recounting her legendary love story with her dearly departed Zeyad. "Love takes us to places that allow our selves to blossom. It puts an end to our beastly selfishness. We stop being just ourselves and become a part of another. It transforms us from raging bulls into sacrificial lambs. It unleashes our primitiveness, and through it we can reach God, the Creator. Our cells regenerate and we try as hard as we can to be sweeter and better in the eyes of our loved ones."

Suddenly she broke down in tears. I approached her gently and hugged her close. I knew how much she needed love and how much thrummed inside her that she needed to share. I passed her a tissue and she wiped her eyes, saying, "You have enough to deal with." Then, again in English, she added sarcastically, "Still, baby, life is good." She then started laughing. I knew she was holding onto her grief by making fun of it and separating it from her reality, watching it from a distance, mocking fate, determined to ridicule her wounds to avoid feeling their pain.

Hala was locked into a struggle with her suffering. She badly wanted to overcome it with her usual stubbornness and persistence. Experience taught her that she had to fight tooth and nail against her bad luck, so as not to be crushed by life. Thousands of hardships, struggles, and sacrifices piled atop her body, encasing her in a shell of coldness and cruelty.

She had to care for herself as you would a child. And she had to suppress the painful feeling that she had created a terrible hell, and that part of her transparency remained trapped in the shadows because she was a man and woman in one body.

Her only obsession was not to be surprised by loss as she had been in her relationship with Ahmad. After their romance came to an end, she trampled over everything: the good and the bad. Hala fled from wounds she had anticipated, because she knew how bad reality was and people's ability to give up what they loved for what their societies deemed important, or to evade responsibility because love in our lives is substantially linked to ourselves and not to the Other. She used to believe that no one really cared about love, or even the object of their love, as much as owning the person. Thus, relationships are always established at the expense of one of the parties; we always forget that love is a living being that, to be complete, needs care like a newborn child. It is not an end in itself, but rather the sea, which we dip into to renew both parties. Otherwise the curtain falls over the fairy tale that we claim links us, and conceals our disappointment behind it.

After her husband passed away, she rejected the idea of getting into another relationship. She was absorbed by grief, stripped of her strength, and unable to care for her child, who had no one but her. She needed a man in her life to reawaken her femininity and therefore also her sense of motherhood, so she would stop being just a burden. But she compared herself, and everyone else, to her late husband.

The difference between him and these others created a deep rift in her soul. She even made excuses, fought with men without feeling guilty, or imagined flaws in them so she wouldn't fall in love with them. This one ate too much, this one not enough, this one was too active, this one not active enough and other unconvincing details. She did like to feel attractive, to seduce men, but it was as if she were looking to be desirable more than the subject of anyone's desire. She had casual relationships and quickly ended them. She swore to me that they were the reason—that no one had succeeded in capturing her heart and making her stay with him.

"No one but my son deserves my love," she affirmed. I was fully aware that her true love for her late husband was what prevented her from indulging in any new relationship. If any man wanted to get through to her, he'd first have to navigate through that narrow crossing called Zeyad and swim through that passageway to learn how to surpass him.

"Please, love will come on its own soon, if it's meant to be there at all," she went on to say. Then she asked me to tell her about Rabih. I started to tell her about my fear of losing him. I don't know where that fear even came from. I showed her what was left of the bruises that Sami had given me, and she cursed him. I knew that she was asking herself what would make a woman put up with all of this harm being done to her. She was convinced that I needed to act and do something about my husband's beatings and insults. Hala's presence in my life gave me strength, and I saw in her a different model of woman than those I'd always lived among. She made me want to take charge of my life, even if it was just once, and make choices about what I myself wanted, not to simply please others.

I looked at Hala and asked her if my pain would ever end. She stared at me for a while and then told me to look at her son. She pointed at the child and said, "This little child has inhaled illness and disease ever since his lungs first breathed air. Every day he sees his friends devouring bread and chocolate, but he has to inject himself with insulin between classes at school. Look at him laughing! He not only has physical handicaps and deprivation, but death stole his father from him. He has no man in his life, no father to guide him, play water guns with him, or make him a kite. When he lies in bed at night, he still calls out to me to come and be next to him. During those long nighttime hours, I feel him sweat, toss and turn, and then curl into me to protect him. After his father passed away, I couldn't find work. You know how my father is chronically unemployed and dependent on me? I couldn't even pay for his medications. Everyone disavowed me when I was at my weakest point. Long nights passed with me totally powerless. But despite all of this suffering I experienced, I am in a better place now. I still hope for a better future for my son. Perhaps your suffering has not yet ended, maybe you're going to live through even worse circumstances than those you've already been through. This is the sad, miserable reality that we live in. But, my friend, even if you are unable to change the world, you can change yourself. Learn to love yourself. Free yourself of feelings of guilt toward that beast you live with. You are haunted by fear, my girl. Don't you see how your skinny body trembles in fear when he speaks to you? You aren't cheating on him, Sahar. You're betraying the misery you live with every day. You're peering out at life through a very narrow opening and freeing yourself with Rabih. You dream of change, and of love. Aren't you doing all of this to feel love, even if it is in constrained conditions?"

I listened to Hala and I watched how she sipped her coffee with pleasure. She passed her tongue over the little coffee cup, pressed her lips against the rim hard, and then smiled. I imagined all of the hardships she'd experienced in her life, which gave her the maturity that her body exuded. Clearly, she had amassed a rich sexual history with men over the years.

Hala first experienced sorrow at a young age. Her mother passed away when she was young, and she and her three siblings lived with their father, who rarely worked. The children, more often than not, had to rely on relatives in order to have their basic needs met. Poverty was Hala's constant companion before she even knew what the word meant. The only thing that helped her and her siblings was that her father owned a small apartment in the Abi Samra area. This meant they had a place to shelter in.

Hala was like a swamp of memories of painful events and misfortunes she'd endured. Her older brother, Ibrahim, who joined various Islamic movements in his adolescence, gave her brutal beatings. This began one fall in the early 1980s. A group calling itself the Tablighi-Jamaat entered their home when Hala was not yet nine years of age.

This group visited their house in the wake of their mother's death. The men's elegant manners helped them to recruit her older brother. As the days passed, her brother's new "brothers" started coming by regularly. For all intents and purposes, their father was absent and didn't exist. He passed hours in silence staring out the window, listening to an old cassette tape playing Umm Kulthum on a loop, puffing on cheap Cedars cigarettes which he smoked two packs of daily. Or else he lounged around at a nearby cafe with other unemployed men like himself.

This religious group really took shape in poor neighborhoods like theirs after first appearing on the ground in Lebanon in 1975. It took the Prophet's birthday celebrations as the date to start its work in the field, with a massive demonstration through the streets of Tripoli, carrying Islamist-jihadist slogans on placards.

At the time, the demonstration was armed. It was launched from Abi Samra, led by Islamist forces under the banner of "Jundallah (Soldiers of God)" to serve as an outlet for the pent-up Islamic sentiment. When they first emerged, these groups represented the sectarian situation, a response to extreme right-wing forces like the Phalangists, the National Liberals (al-Ahrar), the Guardians of the Cedars, and others. They were advisers to those defending the Palestinian cause and sometimes allied themselves with left-wing parties and forces, until the Syrian "Arab Deterrent Force" entered Tripoli.

From what people were saying in the back alleys, the complicity of some of the dominant groups facilitated the Syrians' entry into the city. This prompted the Jundallah group to stop working alongside those forces and announce the dissolution of their organization for lack of a fundamental, Islamic, legal motivation to continue this jihad for the sake of God.

Public actions by Islamic groups on behalf of the Syrian security regime declined in the 1980s. The negative effects of the regime could be seen on the torn-up city streets, which were filled with intimidation, humiliation, and persecution.

The Tablighi Jamaat gradually lured in Ibrahim. Their father was very weak and had no authority over his children. Hala soon noticed the changes in her brother, who had always been conscientious about his studies and worked diligently to remain at the top of his class. This aged Hala. She was a child watching a frustrated father suffering from an inconsolable heartbreak, and a brother searching for a role model as intense and solid as the men who visited them.

For a long time, she just stood behind the door observing them. They said prayers, asked for mercy on their mother's soul, and incited her brother to curse his miserable failure of a father, who made his own misery and excruciating agony worse day after day. It is as if desolation stretches out in front of a person who takes identical, never-ending steps that lead where they don't want to go, so that their anguish and worry only increase when they plunge in.

To his sister, who loved him very much, Ibrahim seemed more and more like a drug addict. She tried repeatedly to get close to him, to find out what was going on inside him, but she failed. Fear and sorrow condemned her to experience how people can find themselves in a quagmire of pain because the connection between them and the Other person feels broken. She contemplated her father and her brother: the former soaked in sorrow, the latter feeding off hatred so strong that even his features changed.

Ibrahim started coming back home in the middle of the night and leaving at dawn. A few times he was gone all night. The neighbors said he was training to take up arms in battle. Hala refused to believe it, even as her brother started going missing for days at a time. Once she tried to get her father to search for him. After they left home, they had to cross a checkpoint of the Arab Deterrent Forces. They beat her father in plain sight. Without any justification, one of the officers started butting him in the stomach with his Kalashnikov until he collapsed. Her servile father simply got up and went back home with his daughter, cursing Ibrahim, their country, the war, deterrence, and the state. After that, he took to his chair next to the window for a full week, waiting for his son to return. When he did, his father took one painful look at him and spat on the ground.

Ibrahim erupted like a raging bull and attacked him. When Hala, weeping and screaming, tried to pull on the edges of the white robes Ibrahim had shown up in, he beat her, too.

After that, they didn't see Ibrahim or hear anything about him. Hala searched in vain for him all over the house. She reached a point of despair. She sat in her room, shook her head, and looked around with tears in her eyes, trying to spot some mark Ibrahim had left behind. She curled up in that warm, lovely spot where they used to sit together for hours, before the preachers persuaded him to abandon his life and forsake his sister.

She pulled Ibrahim's big cloth handkerchief out of the closet and used it to wipe her tears. She kissed it several times and held it tight against her heart. Tears poured out from her beautiful round eyes, under her delicate eyelashes once again. If she had seen her own face, she would have been shocked by the pale pain that showed on it, tears leaving her pretty face puffy and pink.

Hala never learned how Ibrahim disappeared or what became of him. She heard that he'd become one of the religious mujahideen who were awaiting an opportunity to embrace death and martyrdom. Several years after he'd disappeared, people in the neighborhood told her that he'd gone to Iraq for jihad. According to those close to him, a desire to die a hero for the sake of God and not a failure like his father almost ripped him apart. After that whole period had passed, Hala had reached a point of almost pure hatred for her brother for abandoning her and going off without ever considering her fate.

Hala's memory was more like a collective memory. It had suffered from shock and was easily paralyzed by turmoil, if exposed to unexpected outside aggression. She was denied the existence of a hopeful or even delightful reality by discovering the truth.

She lived in a state of shock, burying devastating events deep in her memory, replacing them with jokes and cynicism.

Like Tripoli's memory, Hala's memory had bright and dark impulses, and some that temporarily disappeared from history because no one wanted them back. Whenever painful events occur, societies and people bury them deep down, so that they can adjust gradually to the atrocities they've just experienced. It took a long period of work before Hala was able to disclose her suffering, before the woes that had afflicted her turned into the subject of analysis. Exactly like me today.

Even after events in the city calmed down, she still expected Ibrahim to come back. Her life was a perpetual struggle: to pay her educational expenses, to care for her siblings, to bear the burden of her father's sorrow, and to protect herself from her merciless surroundings. No one cared if her clothes were torn, if she went to sleep hungry, or perhaps even if she died alone in her bed.

At fifteen, Hala's breasts started to fill out, her rear end developed to be high and shapely. Men started falling all over her everywhere, even one of the teachers at Islah High School where she was studying tried to get close to her. Once he asked her to stay after class to get help with one of her assignments, the physics lesson that she was having difficulty understanding. She agreed. That day she went home thinking what a noble, good-hearted teacher Mr. Yasir was. The next day she prepared lunch for her siblings, a bit of potato with onions and cumin. Potatoes were their staple food. Hala was a bit of an artist in making different potato dishes—some days she would do them in the oven, others she'd boil them on the stove and rub them with lemon and olive oil. If they were flush, or a relative had sent them some vegetable oil, she would fry them, and they would devour the golden chips ravenously.

She stayed in the classroom after the final bell rang and all of the students had left. She opened her physics book and prepared her notebook and her blue ink pen. Her teacher Mr. Yasir came in and greeted her, "Welcome, Hala, welcome." Hala laughed shyly, pointing toward her open notebook and saying that she found the embedded mathematical equations in physics difficult. But Mr. Yasir was preoccupied with getting ready to bite into the proverbial apple. He brought his lips in close and kissed Hala hard on the mouth. She rose to her feet quickly, dropping her pen as she stood. She then closed her book and slapped him across the face with it. He couldn't slap her back, so he threw the book on the ground and tried to back her into a corner. Every time Hala told this story, she started laughing hysterically as she described how she kicked him in the balls after he cornered her against the blackboard. She told us how he narrowed his eyes, saying, "You slutty bitch. You act all pure with your ass and boobs stuck up like that!" Hala spat in his face and went back home feeling extremely disappointed in Mr. Yasir, a dirty old man with no morals.

Her tears mingled with the cumin potatoes as she cooked. She had to stop eating to blow her nose and wipe her eyes with a tissue. Later, she opened her physics book and read the same paragraph over and over again for hours, like it was a puzzle that she'd never be able to solve. She kept seeing her teacher's face in the pages of her book and she felt like his hands might just stretch out through the numbers, letters, and physics equations and grope her. Weeping feverishly, she wondered if she could ever face going back to school again.

After Mr. Yasir gave Hala a failing mark in physics, she made a complaint to the headmaster, informing him that her teacher had sexually harassed her and that she'd refused to give into him and he'd penalized her with a low mark as a result. The headmaster merely chided her, pointing to Mr. Yasir's exemplary educational background and irreproachable moral conduct.

The headmaster shouted at her as he was checking out the curves of her body. She sensed that he was just like the physics teacher, and that trying to actually learn something in this high school was going to be tough and exhausting. Hala left the school and enrolled in an institute to study accounting, but she got sick of that too. Every time she studied, she was reminded of her teacher and headmaster. It became impossible for her to even be around pens and paper. She abandoned knowledge, never to return, even though she always loved to learn. She had to be content with her middle school diploma on which she had received a mark of "very good."

She found work at a shop called Lemara downtown on Azmi Street, the most modern area in town, which sold perfume and women's underwear. She started taking English classes in the afternoon at an institute near her office. She liked studying English, in fact, just as much as the clothes she sold—satin nightdresses, lacy underwear, and the brightly colored thongs and panties she wore over her voluptuous curves. Hala also loved the hot dogs sold in the kiosks lining the street there.

When she was seventeen years old, she fell in love with a boy called Ahmad. He was also studying English. She started seeing him every day. She experienced a wide margin of freedom because of her absent father and two brothers occupied with their own affairs. She told him about things in her life, the clients in the shop, and deliberately described to him how couples came in to pick out lingerie together. She tried to send the message that she wanted to marry him and travel together to foreign countries where they could speak English while eating hot dogs and ice cream. She told him about her teacher Mr. Yasir and the way men unrelentingly pursued her. She was always eager to stress how important her honor and virginity were to her.

She thought that he wouldn't kiss her after she expressed her resentment toward those who coveted her curvaceous body. But he did so at the theater while they were watching the film *Zorro* with Catherine Zeta-Jones and Antonio Banderas. He went even further and slid his hand under her shirt where she'd left two buttons open. He caressed her nipples and pulled on them sensuously. She found herself totally surrendering to his kisses. Her lips melted into his and her tongue plunged into his mouth. It moved in circles that mimicked his, and it experienced a pleasure even greater than that provided by the sandwiches she devoured voraciously. When he got carried away and put his hand in her underwear, she cried out and he quickly removed it.

She didn't want him to come too close to her private parts, so he tried to get her to touch his penis, which she did reluctantly. Soon she got used to stroking it, and she learned how to make him come with her mouth. They used to do this recklessly in the changing room where she worked when her boss wasn't there. She never let him put his hands between her legs; she was determined to remain a virgin. But she didn't mind pleasuring his entire body and helping him ejaculate. She did all of this with a feeling of love and satisfaction. She dreamed of them getting married one day and escaping to a foreign country where everyone spoke English and they would eat as many hot dogs and hamburgers as they liked.

Then one day suddenly he stopped calling her. She was stunned to learn that he'd gotten engaged to a religious girl who wore a hijab. She started calling him every day with no answer until, one day, a girl's voice responded. She told her to stop calling this number because it belonged to her fiancé and she hated it when girls called him. Hala screamed down the phone at her, "You're a whore, you and him both." All Ahmad's fiancée had to do then was hang up the phone, leaving Hala in a state of mourning, phone in hand and line cut off, until her fiery anger and voice returned.

Ahmad stopped coming to English class and completely disappeared from her life. She later learned that he and his religious woman went to Qatar to work in an advertising agency. She bemoaned her unknown future and started to hate both English and the shop where she worked because it reminded her of the boy who she'd made come in the name of love but who then just abandoned her for someone else.

She walked slumped over, heartbroken, through the narrow alleys leading to her house, determined to find another job. She swore never to give any other man the chance to hurt her. Before she let this happen again she would trample over her own heart and let cats and dogs prey on her outdated emotions.

Hala felt that her heart was a scrap of meat surrounded by a pack of dogs all vying to take a piece. She looked at her heart with regret as it was ripped to shreds, feeding those hungry beasts. At times, she felt like scraping it back up. It occurred to her she could throw herself in with them, beat them off of her, and shout at them, "Give me back my heart! Give me back my mother, Ibrahim and Ahmad." But then she remembered again the sheer amount of torment that this last one, and his throbbing penis, as she liked to call it in moments of anger, had caused her. Then she would regain her composure, look at the dogs condescendingly, and continue on her way.

Hala gave up on her dream of living in abroad, teaching English, and becoming a flight attendant flitting from country to country like a bumblebee. She was a butterfly with clipped wings, condemned to remain trapped in the clutches of hideous poverty that had always violated her desires and stacked her disappointments one atop the other.

Her dreams turned to dust until there was nothing left but her fantasies, imagination, and desire to overcome the painful reality that she didn't do justice to the love of her life. Ahmad abandoned her, leaving her with a mutilated dignity that she struggled to preserve. Soon the ghost of Zeyad appeared before her. He wasn't fluent in English and hadn't mastered the fine art of dining on hot dogs, but he was extremely kind and gentle. He had a simple apartment on 200th Street and owned a shop where he worked as a mechanic, repairing cars and at times buying and selling them.

Poverty had etched itself on her features and her stomach had all but exploded from her potato-filled diet. Her very existence exhausted her, and she was fed up with the sight of her father, who offered her nothing. He was simply at home, unemployed, and discontented with the miserly society that had robbed him of his wife. He felt he had too much dignity to endure the humiliation of looking for a job. The bourgeoisie remained his stolen dream; it had betrayed him the moment he gave up his ticket to Europe, and with it, the chance to attain a passport. He would have done this even if it had meant marrying one of the girls over there.

Hala's father had begun his sexual relationship with her mother before they were married and was forced to marry her when she was still a young teenager because she got pregnant. He remembered the look on her face the moment she told him she was pregnant. He felt that she had betrayed him. Were it not for his fear of a scandal and the taint of immorality, he wouldn't have hesitated to ask her to have an abortion. But he couldn't do it. He would have lost his mother's prayers for success. He soon started being plagued by nightmares. He dreamed of an airplane, a child hanging from its wings. This made him stay in his country. His mother repeated prayers for children after this, and then his wife left him alone with four children and unfulfilled dreams. He swore never to marry again, less out of fidelity to his late wife than outrage at death and anger at a country and a city that murdered dreams.

Neither death nor loss were strangers to Hala. She knew both before her husband passed away. She'd inhaled them along with the air of her childhood, just as now she is breathing in the air of loneliness and successive losses. She married Zeyad and convinced herself that love would come after marriage. She thought that even if he didn't speak a foreign language, this man would give her a break from those others who merely coveted her body.

After they were together, she began to love him deeply. She found it sweet that someone would take over and be responsible for her banal, daily affairs. Holding Zeyad by the arm proudly, she would visit her father and make sure to mention how kind he was, as if taking revenge against how cruelly she had been treated under her father's care.

She always dreamed of finding Ahmad, giving him a look of pride, and slapping him to heal from the harm he'd caused her. She imagined informing her brother Ibrahim that a better man than himself had decided to take care of her.

She hoped that Ahmad wasn't happy. She prayed to God that his wife was meek, hideous looking, and depressive. The moment she was abandoned, she kept thinking about how he had accepted what she offered him. He didn't have the courage to tell her he didn't want her. Feelings of rejection assaulted her night after night. She would feel a tingling all over her body and wake up scared in the middle of the night her face awash in bitter tears. She hugged her pillow, burying her face in it, until she dozed off. In the morning, she would find streaks of black kohl smeared on her pillowcase.

Only her marriage to Zeyad saved her from a despair that was like a knife twisting into her back. Her husband took her to the movies, for walks on the corniche every evening, and bought her perfume and other gifts. He even helped her with the housework. He encouraged her to keep studying English after she became pregnant with their son. He taught her to drive a car and promised to take her on a trip to Europe after their child had grown up a bit. But Zeyad wasn't able to keep his promise. Stupid death stole from her once again, leaving her all alone with her son, his illness, and a feeling of being unable to complete her path in life.

But Hala continued down the arduous path she found herself on. She had to put some distance between herself and her reality and find the irony in her tragedy. Life is like a great farce that we can't control and thus all we can do is look for a little joy, so that we can anesthetize ourselves against the horrors of this world. She decided to live on as little as possible. No, to live and take care of herself and her son was not her decision, but rather her destiny.

After she became a widow, men flocked to her from every direction. But she had sworn never to fall into the trap called love ever again. She felt like they all came to her simply because they wanted to have sex with her. She repeated on a loop, "They only want to sleep with you."

"Why don't they tell me that they want to hook up with me? It would make things clearer. But they insist on pretending that they care about my English lessons and my diligent, hardworking personality." She would say this with irony, as a comment on how trivial people could be.

She compared these men to members lined up in a long queue waiting for free sex, men she would sleep with and then leave. "I betray them before they betray me, I abandon them before they leave me," she would repeat, blowing her cigarette smoke out and watching it drift off. It was as if she were staring into her soul, which was evaporating with the every new lover she added to her list.

Hala finished her English lessons after Zeyad passed away and found work at an insurance company. She was able to secure a modest income, which helped her avoid the humiliation of asking her husband's relatives to pay for her son's treatments. She started reading a lot of novels and other books in English, which added a broad element of culture to her life experience, which consisted of flesh and blood, as she used to put it. The stories she read took her to different worlds, to civilizations that she would have visited if she had held onto her dream of being a flight attendant. Sometimes I felt that she was trying to experience life through her multiple relationships, as if the scars she carried were badges of honor despite the sheer pain attached to them.

Hala had experienced the limits of human brutality. Many times, she endured this voluntarily, testing life or desiring to enter the forbidden unknown, which was part of my imaginary world. She dared to mix in real life with those who I only knew in my imagination. She embodied a will to live and the price you pay for desire. But she was strong, and she persevered. I watched her save up money to chase the scraps of her dream—setting up a little institute for teaching English in her house.

CHAPTER 23

"What does unfaithful mean, Mama?" Dunya asked me once while I was in the midst of washing dishes. I raised my eyebrows and looked into her face, brimming with sweet innocence. I asked her where she'd learned this word and she replied that she'd heard it on television. Her answer relieved the heavy weight crushing my chest. I shouted at her to never ever repeat this word again. She kept insisting that I explain it to her and so I slapped her hard across her face. My fingers went numb against my daughter's cheek. For a split second, I hated her and myself. Hearing her question about the meaning of the word "unfaithful" immediately made me feel as if my dress had slipped off of my body, that I was standing naked in my kitchen, and that any minute her father would come in and have sex with me in front of her.

Dunya ran to her room sobbing. I pulled out a chair and sat down. I could no longer stand. I started thinking about how tough I'd become, like midwives or women who wash the dead and prepare them for burial. The dishes I was washing turned into corpses piled up one atop the other. My hand suddenly slipped and I dropped and broke one. The glass shattered and

Dunya kept crying. Like an automaton, as if I were another woman, cruel and moronic, I bent to gather up the smashed plate.

When a shard of glass pierced my hand and blood began to drip onto the floor, it struck me how wretched I'd become. Drip drop. As the spots of blood flowed from my hand, I was surprised at how consistent they were. Drip drop. Like a scene in a film I'd seen a few days earlier. The heroine had run over a child on a bike with her car and didn't even stop to check on him. As for me, I would have left an entire people crushed under the car. Somehow I had become Marie Antoinette, only sympathizing with tyrants and other hateful people.

The part of me that glowed and laughed like a child was no longer there. My heart could no longer take so much suffering. I covered my face with my hand. Blood mixed with the tears streaming down my cheeks and I wanted to wipe myself away completely. I gathered up all my strength and went into my daughter's room. I told her, "Sometimes, Dunya, we are afraid to speak about our hidden feelings even to those close to us for fear of doing harm to them or ourselves. We have to pretend that we are something we are not in order to impress them. Unfaithful means not telling the truth and lying to those around us, not saying what we feel for fear of other people's reactions."

"Why don't we tell the truth, Mom?"

"Because it will cost us."

"I never want to be unfaithful to anyone."

"You won't, dear Dunya, you always say what you are feeling."

Dunya laughed. I kissed her and hugged her close. My children were the only real things in my life. They are love. They're all the love that lifted the oppression and hatred I'd suffered, and they'd helped me to endure the sheer amount of emotion within me. Meanwhile, the way I'd treated my young daughter made me feel like a version of my mother. I tried to atone for my wrongdoing in every way I could think of, to make her feel that I was there for her—to listen to her and support her. My memories took me back to my childhood home and the gloomy atmosphere that pervaded it.

My father left for Kuwait after his dreams of revolution collapsed. He was a useless romantic who would stitch together dreams, weaving tragedy into them. He liked to play the hero. He spent hours talking about his memories of the revolution and how he fought in the war against Israel. He closed his eyes and talked about his comrade Yusuf whose hands were soaked in his blood when an enemy bullet penetrated his body. My father got carried away with his dreams of revolution and a new renaissance, while my mother remained mired in deep sorrow. For a while she tried to be a part of her husband's world. She felt sympathy for a time when the Cause was real, unlike today, when everything had simply turned into a game of mutual interests.

"Poor people really have gotten the wrong end of the stick," she always said. But my father would look at her disdainfully as if he wanted her to stay out of politics and go back to the kitchen, whose smells pervaded the whole house and got on his nerves.

My father wasn't very kind, especially to my mother. He deliberately left his dirty socks on the floor in the hall for her to pick up. We would wake up to her shouting, loudly, denouncing him as a despicable bourgeois. "Who the hell does that son of a bitch think he is?" she would bellow.

My mother took advantage of his frequent absences to utter these profanities, denouncing his lineage from his ancestors right down to his yet unborn descendants. But deep inside, she loved him. She longed for him to be close to her again and fulfill her pent-up desires. She dreamed of having a name like Anna or Olga and being as graceful as the Russian women who filled Beirut's cabarets, pouring into the capital from every corner to steal Lebanese men away from the local women.

My mother was sure that behind his wishy-washy liberal veneer, my father was actually macho as a rooster. She knew roosters; they stood atop the coop and beckoned to the chickens to come close when they wanted them. She used to say he was a rooster who only liked to crow. She wondered what he was doing with his penis and how he was releasing his sexual energy, which he had withheld from her for so long.

The contours of his fingers that had once touched her body now seemed almost like fantasies flickering in the bed where she spent many sleepless nights. My mother denied her femininity and gave up her dreams of sleeping with someone; she was ravaged by her need for a man's body as darkness cast its shadow over the world. She was a deep well exploding with desire. He didn't notice any of the powders and creams she used on her skin, her intentionally bright, vividly colored lipstick, the perfume she sprayed on her body and clothes, or the red, blonde, and dark colors that she dyed her hair. He didn't care about any of this. Now that femininity has become an elusive, unattainable dream for her, I could swear that she regrets not having cheated on him, never taking up the offer of one of the many men who had flirted with her and praised her unique beauty.

CHAPTER 24

As a child I used to love crawling onto my father's lap, so he'd hold me in his arms. Sometimes he'd even surprise me with a rare show of kindness, shattering the rough and stiff image my mother used to condemn him for. Eventually I would get bored and slip out between his legs and run away laughing.

The fondest memory I have of my father is him carrying me down to the shop to buy sweets. Why is there such a great divide between the two of us now? How am I so distant when I'm his only daughter? How did I replace my father with Sami, as the main man in my life?

When he left to work in Kuwait, I felt separated from a place I already didn't belong. I projected my need to belong to a man on my father, even if this belonging wasn't conscious and had been cultivated in my private inner Self, which I refused to admit.

I remember that I spent many hours at school crying because I missed my father, so much so that the teacher sometimes had to call my mother to come and take me home. Angry as usual, my mother would come with a frown on her face, pulling me by the hand, throwing me into a taxi, and ordering me to stop crying.

She would smoke a cigarette and blow out the smoke, angry and anxious. Did my mother miss him too and wish she could break down and cry like me? Did my mother's womanhood weep? But she preferred restraint and never indulged. She was a wise woman. She knew he was in Kuwait to give us a decent life. She also knew that his absence was no different from him being present, and it caused less torment. With her present-absent man far away, my mother remained prisoner to a wounded memory. This memory was her husband's desire for her, which, like the light in his eyes, had waned like a dying candle. She could no longer bring him happiness, even for a moment; indeed she left this memory barren, desiccated, and untouched by any love or feeling.

One day after picking me up from school, my mother took me with her to her sister's house, where she detached herself from me completely and left me to cry on my own. She spent hours sitting in the kitchen with her sister, who was a good cook and always bragged about being a "master of the culinary arts." I remained trapped between longing for my father and feeling neglected by my mother.

I sat contemplating a large bowl filled with fruit, the grapes hanging over the sides, while remaining in my spot and attempting to attract my mother's attention. My auntie brought me a plate of hot cooked food and I consumed it joylessly. Then I went back to crying. My weeping confounded and enraged my mother, and she swore she would never pick me up from school again. She dragged me to the door before I'd finished my food, and managed to keep her composure in front of the taxi driver, shooting me harsh looks that told me I would have a lot to account for when we reached home. Alone in my room, I stared at my father's photo, wishing I had gone with him to Kuwait. But I knew how far away it was. I traced my pinky finger around the circular picture frame, touching my father's face, bringing him back from the country of his exile.

My features had changed a lot by the time he returned the first time. I had grown taller, my breasts had filled out, and I'd lost a bit of weight. My new look frightened my father. His daughter was no longer a little girl. He could no longer carry me, I could no longer slip in between his legs. He looked at me in a strange way, as if I were no longer his daughter. I had become a young woman, and it confused him and made him feel awkward. He no longer knocked before he came into my room. I felt embarrassed by my new role and felt like I should hide my newfound femininity from him so I could go back to being his little girl, who he could hold on his lap and who could hide under the sofa.

How distant those days seem, when I thought that I would stay Daddy's little girl forever. I thought he'd always be that wolf ferociously defending his pup. Now that I'm in my thirties, I've started thinking about all the lost days I spent without my own identity. I could never get past my being my father's daughter or Sami's wife. And now here I am, trying to be something special and wonderful. I dreamed of fairy tales and fantasylands, and I wound up as someone's mistress.

My passion and faith in the dreams that my father passed down to me never wavered. I picked them up from his complaints without him knowing and cultivated them as specters that pursued me. I am that little girl running through fields on her tiny feet, stealing glances at the sun and the ingenuity of creation, totally engrossed in every breath of air she inhales, listening carefully to the soul of nature, becoming nothing. To become subordinate to Sami, I skipped over my own existence as if it meant nothing. A doll. How did I lose my connection to my own free and rebellious soul, which flowed from deep within life itself? I had been determined to design new houses for the entire city, but I wound up working as an insurance broker because I had no experience in any other area.

How hard did I laugh when I applied for a job in my field and the only reply I received was that, ten years after leaving school and in absence of any job experience, my degree was meaningless? I wanted to reply that I had a degree in the good behavior of battered women—how best to absorb humiliation and subordination. As a condition of my acceptance into that course I had several years of self-denial, and here I am today with a rage inside myself that cannot be calmed. My skin remembers severe beatings and my subservience, thinking that I would relieve my husband of his stress and short temper.

I collapsed onto the sofa while bouncy tunes on the radio seeped into the silence. I started shivering, my muscles reacting involuntarily, rising and falling without me being there at all.

Sometimes, when I was getting undressed, I would be struck by a sudden urge to call Rabih, only to realize how far away he was. I felt that all my sexual fantasies could no longer satisfy my desire to be with him and I burst into tears. Later, I would chain smoke, pacing up and down the house like a prisoner moving around in a cell that can barely accommodate them. Had it not been for my children—that I could still touch Dunya's soft skin and observe little Tareq's mind, which shouldn't have to ponder these kinds of questions—I wouldn't have been able to overcome the grief weighing on my chest. When I got ahold of myself, I fumbled around, making silly jokes and teasing them tenderly, hoping to hear them say that they loved me. Only then could I restore my self-worth from my wounds and the scars that surfaced upon my soul like red spots on smallpox victims.

I recalled how Sami would mock me when I spoke up and told him I couldn't stand living with him anymore and that if he didn't stop beating me, we could both face grave consequences. But he was convinced that he was always right. During this time, I was like a woman handcuffed in some kind of perverse game. I was being punished for having an unbounded imagination, banned from the neighborhood and the city.

Sami used to order me to do all kinds of things. Once he told me that I should leave the laundry outside on the line for three whole days so that it could soak in the sun. I remember how he rubbed my fingers in his hand, pulling on them jokingly and asked, "Does it hurt yet?" At the beginning of our marriage, he would stare at me as I watched television. If there was a scene when the main characters kissed, he would throw himself on top of me as if I were the enemy. He would look at me uncertainly and tug at me, pulling me towards him; one hug would never suffice, and having sex once wasn't enough to satiate him.

Before I married him, I thought Sami was weighed down by the feeling that he didn't possess me, and this is what pushed him to act so ferociously. But now I remember how he used to rip off my clothes and push me down onto the sofa to corner me in between the armrests. I know that he was possessed by one thing—he had to have me completely, take my autonomy and control what was inside me.

This is how all the elder men in our community acted toward those classified as of a lower rank, like Hala and Rabih. This was in line with the authority vested in them, whether their powers were social, political, or religious. In place of the old shop selling rugs, chaos reigned. The old ruins and monuments lost their splendor and were replaced by ugly concrete shops. Every place knew at least one tyrant—husbands, rulers, or jailers. Victims were surrounded by ugliness until it inhabited them, and they were unable to look at themselves or their well-clad leaders. Heads bowed, they submitted to what they were told was the way of the world. The alleyways that were not totally inhabited by misery were merely anticipating their destiny. Sorrow, ignorance, and collective humiliation surrounded the city center, which was clogged with taxis, workers, beggars, and shoe shiners. The city was like an attractive woman who'd been dressed in rags, or a burqa, to make her disappear, because the only thing allowed was suppression.

Even though we were living in the most modern part of Tripoli, we always looked like an imported version of deprivation. We were the class that had arrived—we had new buildings, spacious apartments with large, contemporary furnishings, rugs and carpets covering as much of the floor as possible, and photographs. But our class hadn't shaken off our small and limited gray-and-white lives, closed off within ourselves, our mirrors insidiously and guiltily reflecting our pact with nothingness. We'd given up our freedom for progress that might not even happen during our lifetimes.

Just as I had contradictory feelings toward my husband—on the one hand kindness, guilt, and defeat, and on the other, hatred, sorrow and the desire to flee—I had similar mixed emotions about the city. It was like selling a mortgaged apartment and waiting for a good price to pay off the debt and secure an amount substantial enough to pay for necessary expenses for a certain amount of time. This would guarantee a subdued departure.

I realized too late that he wasn't spying on me out of jealousy but a desire to appropriate me completely. He would look at me with wide, child-like eyes if I found him looking through my clothes or rummaging through my things. He would make his voice completely neutral, equidistant from lies and the truth, and state that what was mine was his. He would then go back to searching around, plundering anything of mine that he possibly could. Sami liked to acquire everything. His mother taught him to always cancel out others in order to preserve his own place. I asked him to give me a little space to allow me to miss being with him. But he never gave me any chance to miss him or long for him. His way of loving me made me hate him. Now I can feel how ridiculous and even absurd his love is. For him, the private is public and I am that private. I am that illusion that he tried to hold in his hand, not to keep it but to strangle it. Years passed and I felt guilty because I could never fully be that illusion, the trophy that validated his selfishness and excessive vanity. Years passed and I was shackled by what they call love.

At the beginning of our relationship, I didn't know that he was haunted by a mirage. Now when I think about why I married him, I know that I also was silly. I married him to escape my mother's pain, which plagued me night after night. I married him in search of a father, having grown distant from my own amidst the noise of daily life. He married me, wanting to extract me from my Self to become a ship that he owned, one whose sails he could tear apart if he wanted and even leave out in a storm if he so desired. I was a boat he rode in his imagination, struggling against the waves that pounded against me. Can love blossom in a city inhabited by such selfishness? Can love grow in a garden tended by the hands of a spoiled child?

Perhaps he didn't love me and I didn't love him. Perhaps love is simply a delusion we cling to for fear of losing our identity, one we use to show we can have influence. Perhaps it exceeds everything. The opposite of the opposite; the contrary of the contrary. Absolute faith in the impossible. Love is something that transcends our innocence, life's boring details, and the scent of death that pervades married people's apartments—the frenzied desire that the Other partner be their safety net, a lifeline that enables them to cross to the other side. After they've crossed then they suddenly cast a net in search of new fish, higher yields, and different desires.

Within the chaos of our absurd existence, we fall prey to boredom and forget what is really important. We hold our breath. We sweat for the most trivial reasons. We hurt others whose eyes beg us for mercy. Love resembles love and disappointments continue within us. We discover whether the Other, who we created from our own desires and according to our own measure, is broad or narrow. Perhaps we've gained a few extra kilos, or sometimes we've lost them. This desire to lose myself in the Other has always led me to make unrealistic choices. When I think about Sami now, I realize that men are a city of children and we women are a city of dolls. A boy doesn't go looking for a doll. Sometimes he puts it on the shelf; he might forget it there or be bored with it. Other times he hugs her to him and can't sleep without it.

When I try to recall his face, many faces flash before me, as if he were never an individual but a group. For example, I'd see his spinster sister who I started hating even more after she put on the hijab. She'd stare at my hair, wanting to pounce on me and cover it while talking to me condescendingly. There was also his mother, who kowtowed to him and his ever-silent father. He was shackled by his family and he stumbled in front of them, which made him want to assert his authority over me even more. He would deliberately insult me within his mother's earshot, just to put the smile of victory on her lips.

Their nighttime gatherings could be described in no other way but boring. They watched Egyptian or Syrian soap operas and indulged in exaggerated reactions if anything bad happened to their favorite characters. For them, Sami was like a soap star who'd married an ordinary woman, a commoner. To them, I was nothing more than a channel they wished they could change. I lost my tolerance for sitting with them, unless it was to observe the comedy in their gatherings. I'd memorize what they said and did and then replay the scenes to Hala when I saw her. Sometimes we acted out their strange exploits with each other in exaggerated ways, and we'd dissolve into laughter.

We entertained ourselves imagining his spinster sister holding a picture of me and comparing us. We fabricated scenarios in which she'd go to séances to try to conjure up jinn to get rid of me or reveal how I'd managed to get married when she hadn't. Hala often said she wouldn't be surprised to learn one day that his mother wasn't fully human, but rather a creature possessed by demons that enjoyed taking lives. She even mocked Sami for relying on his mother to sneak him the sweets that gave him additional energy to fuel his beatings.

She used to say to me in English, "Why do you put up with their shit? Break free, honey, while you still can!" Whenever she spoke English, she'd pull her hair back like a movie star. Laughing, she'd say, "Out of all of my many lovers, not one had a family like his." I asked her why she didn't stick with just one man.

"Not until a man comes along who shakes me to the very core of my being. Believe me, if there is such a person out there, I'll leave aside all of my failed attempts to convince myself that I'm just looking for transient pleasure in the wake of so many men," she answered with confidence.

Hala was always in need of a lover. She tried to use these flings to become indifferent, to stifle her extreme sensitivity and the love that was destroying her. She met them by chance. Every time, she convinced them—and forced herself to believe as well—that she didn't need them. She would leave them on a whim, only to discover too late which one of them might have had the gift of perfect rhythm, or of understanding what she was saying, even if it did not match her actions.

She had an adventurous flirtation with the first man she knew after her husband. He always spoke to her about the absolute state of abandon that a person experiences, which you can't blame either on the presence or absence of God. She decided to experience a pleasure that she faded into until she vanished completely. She believed in this experiment until the man became obsessed. He got too attached to her and clung to her every time she pulled away, completely disregarding all of his own theories about abandonment and getting lost in love. She had also fallen in love with him, but felt herself trapped in a maze that he wanted her to adapt to within the variables of time.

Hala drew close and then pulled away, came close again and then pulled back. He drowned her in all of his philosophies and theories, and soon enough she fled him.

She soon realized that he was simply an eccentric man who lacked the ability to make life decisions for himself and became mired in unrealistic dreams of the future. Hala became overwhelmed by an unrivaled feeling of boredom that developed into a kind of contempt. She escaped, wrapping a sheet around her body to conceal herself. A believer in the theory of abandonment, the man pursued her for some time. But she turned the page, bitterly and sorrowfully, because his behavior proved the opposite of what he said.

After a while, in an attempt to get right back to it, she ended up with a religiously committed man. Her new lover was extremely kind, which over time came to seem more like a sort of pity. Pity leaves a person in the position of being a spectator and is unfair to the one being pitied.

Hala made him feel victorious and lucky to his very depths. It was as if God and religion had provided him with a family unlike hers, because he was the chosen one. When they were finished having sex, he'd launch into disconcerting conversations about what was permitted and forbidden in religion, halal and haram. He lectured her on the evils of disrespecting herself. She once asked him, "Aren't you doing the same thing?"

"But you don't mind."

"Because I want to be near you."

"Me too."

"Why are you comparing us?"

"No, no, it's different."

"How is it different?"

"Why so many questions?"

"Because I want to know. Would you have loved me more if I hadn't had sex with you?"

"I don't think so."

"Don't you desire me?"

"Of course, a lot!"

"Don't you want me to desire you?"

"Yes, so much."

"Then why do you speak as though you want to limit my desires?"

"I don't know if that's what I want…"

"Because desire is haram? Forbidden?"

Hala's lover was silent for a long time. He then tried to wrap her in his arms, but she slipped away from him. She said, "I'm wild and unruly; I don't understand why you are trying to kill my passion for life. You all want to be in love with me in the dark, but you kill me when I come near the light. Is this not forbidden?"

Her lover grew silent once more. This was the silence when there is no need for sound, because anything that might be said would make no difference.

"The damage is already done," she said in English.

He tried to convince her to meet him for dinner, but she abandoned him quickly, cursing the loneliness that drove her into the arms of predators who projected their duplicity onto her out of hatred for her liberation, the depths of which they could never reach.

Her succession of lovers resembled exaggerated theatrical characters, frightened creatures trying to push Hala into a sad quagmire that might break her or demand she be weak and frail as the price for her desire for spontaneity. Contrary to what we claim, no one wants to expand the horizons of their mind, reckoning with its difficult impulses, only to find weakness there. Then it is all for naught. The need for the other shouldn't be an end in itself, but rather the natural, gentle, deep flow of life. Hala was someone propelled by lust, who could live at the edge of the abyss despite the difficulties, loneliness, and pain.

All of these experiences refined Hala's personality and gave her the power and ability to capture life's little details. She wasn't able to handle death like I was, nor was she convinced that love should mean insults, beatings, and torture. She always imagined it to be the contrary. Love was bringing together opposites—the soft and the harsh. She strove for that kind of balance though she didn't know its actual purpose. Her love for life, her desire for reinvention and to remain open to all possibilities came before what she said. Nothing was impossible for Hala. She even planted the idea in her son, whose illness dominated his life, that if God takes something from you, he will reward you with many other kinds of blessings. According to her, we can't have everything. God bestows his blessings with a plan, even if life seems cruel and unfair. He is the Absolute, and if we truly believe in him, our main concern will not be if he is watching us having sex. We will be convinced on our own if the hijab is a divine duty or a human choice. If we follow his path and pursue our dreams, we will discover the truth of his existence.

For Hala, God is love, all love. He is the light that filtered through the room when she was a girl, where her twisted orphaned arms and her father's disappointments resided. She said that God was there even in the fabric of our clothes, in the pores of our skin. Hala was proud of her mistakes, her remorse and repentance, and everything that made her feel alive. According to her, if we don't make mistakes, we will never know the blessings to come.

"This doesn't mean that I never gave up on my faith in the most critical moments, but Sahar, my faith never gave up on me. It's my little boy, my son, who made the seeds of generosity sprout within me even during days of drought," she often said.

I would respond, "You're really strange, Hala!" When I'm in bed thinking about how strange my friend is, I try to believe that happiness perhaps resides in a hot dog that you eat with gusto. Then I realize once again that I can't ever be happy because then I won't be myself.

I can recall everything she's ever told me about her painful childhood. I can picture her holding tight to her teddy bear because she was all alone, her mother far away. I see her as a little girl weighed down by poverty, deprivation, and premature responsibilities. Sometimes I imagine suffering trailing behind her like a shadow. I watch her playing with her child, holding his hands and kissing them. I observe her speaking on the phone with mockery and disdain to her many admirers. I wonder if she's lost faith in people, in finding someone to hold her hand. Are most people more or less the same as my friend Hala claims? If we really want to be realistic, should we expect that no one will be our savior? Do we flee to the Other so that we don't have to face up to our troubles, or the cruelty of this existence that makes trying to communicate with each other seem impossible?

Hala's happiness, a large part of what she calls joy, stems from her freedom. Her hope emerges from despair, just as jasmine flowers blossom white from within the clutches of green. I'm insignificant because I take life's more serious path, just as a table should always be placed on the left side of a sitting room, walls ivory colored, and bills all unpaid. There's no room for change. In my house we eat regular meals, clothes are ironed and folded, there are no stains on the children's clothes. Everything is as it should be. My husband even has sex with me according to our usual customs and procedures. Even our boredom is orderly. Nothing penetrates our organized life except his uncontrollable bouts of rage.

I didn't break with our expected meals or our expected life, except when I was cheating on Sami—when everything unexpected got into me. I didn't realize how far my life had declined until I let myself experience this. I left Sami's world and allowed Sahar to be herself. The problem was that I was "me" when I spent time with my lover, and I went back to being "them" the rest of the time. I retreated back into the mold that has been assigned to women since the beginning of time.

When I confronted myself alone, I knelt on the ground, bit the edge of the wooden bed, and saw the Sahar who was as crippled as a worn-out steel girder. I reached out to her and found the ground damp with her tears. I used to tremble, not because I was cold, but out of fear. Blue chills would overtake my body. Images came back to haunt me. I felt like I was a whore, just as Sami always said I was. I was a prostitute, liar, and hypocrite and I should be stoned for it. I had violated the memory of the chaste women of my village and contaminated it by cheating on my husband. I had besmirched them with my infidelity, and they besmirched me by teaching me infidelity itself before I even knew it. They violated me by teaching me that it's OK for a man to insult and beat his wife.

CHAPTER 25

So immersed was I in my own infidelity that I didn't realize that death might steal away my auntie Samia. She was the only woman whose features I had preserved in my mind. Somehow I didn't really think that death would dig its claws into us. When I looked in the mirror, I saw my prematurely gray hair, the wrinkles under my eyes, and the grief I'd tried to conceal under makeup. But my aunt was dead. No. I'd forgotten that death exists, and that life has an end.

As I sat in the room packed with mourners, I thought about the details of her house, the things I'd overlooked in the chaos of my own emotions and obsession with searching for the answers to the questions that had plagued me since childhood. There she was with her fragile body, arms sticking out, like a portrait by a blind artist who used a lack of sight to produce something more creative. Though I'd grown used to the notion of her death by this time, I still ran over to where her body lay and kissed her forehead, hands, and feet. I started thinking about how harsh, dry, and abused I'd become. I thought about how I'd neglected to visit her because I was caught up in the chaos of my own life, even though she never once held back her love or good counsel from me. I passed my hands over my auntie's face and touched death. I reconstructed her life, imagining her house decorated with jasmine flowers and the tablecloths that she had embroidered patiently and with great care.

The room was noisy with women who I only then realized how much I hated. They were intruders who'd rushed to get there first and wash the body so they could score points with God. I shouted at them to leave her alone; I screamed and cried hysterically. It struck me how alone she was. She was a woman who ate alone and drank alone. She embroidered tablecloths alone. She watered her garden with water as pure as her soul. She was the most honest of all these women.

As I grew older, she told me, "Sahar, I sleep with my principles. And my principles have nothing to do with a man." When she was younger, my auntie had loved a man called Nabil. But he was poor and didn't match up to her family's requirements, as they were mainly concerned with their connections, lineage, and pride. They forced her to forget getting together with him, as they wanted her to marry a well-off man considered to be a village noble. I've never seen anything like my auntie's principled stance. She refused to marry the man who they'd tried to force on her. She held onto Nabil like you hold a fish by the tail. And in a period when women didn't have the right to say no, my aunt shouted, "Either I marry Nabil or I never marry." My grandfather locked her in the house for two years. Her female relatives weren't even allowed to visit her. But she stayed strong.

"I will not marry a man I do not love," she told her father bravely, even as he beat and slapped her. She stayed locked up at home until my grandfather lost hope that she would ever see reason. His biggest concern was that their neighbors knew that Nabil hadn't taken her virginity. But my auntie no longer wanted to marry Nabil or anyone else. She felt betrayed and heartbroken when they gave her the news that he'd married someone else, having realized that their relationship was impossible. It wasn't so much his marriage that hurt her, but the betrayal of a vow they'd once made to each other. She used to clasp her hands over her belly and declare that her womb would never carry a child. She'd been convinced that Nabil would fight for her to the last breath, but he didn't. "Men are chickens, darling," she used to say with a laugh. "They say that we are cowards, but the best of men can hardly deal with what women deal with all alone."

My auntie refused to marry a man she didn't love, but with the passing of time she realized how bitter loneliness could be. It was difficult to wake up every morning without anybody to share breakfast with, or even the shadow of a man to visit her at night to share a bit of warmth.

"I wanted to have a child, my dear, a son who would look like Nabil—walk like him and talk like him. That's all I wanted." She told me of these things after I'd grown up, and I got to know the women of the village through how she talked about them. They considered her a fool, a spinster, someone who spent her whole life in the garden tending to her plants sometimes giving them water, other times tears.

For these women in the village, she stood as an example for younger women, living proof of the lesson, "Love won't put food on your table." From Samia they learned that spinsterhood was the price to be paid for attempting to forge one's own path in life. Now she was a corpse. All I could do was wonder whether Nabil knew how much she'd loved him, if he knew that she'd kept all the flowers he'd ever given her wrapped up in an ivory-colored scarf. Did he know how much she'd cried, and how many beatings she'd endured to avoid being with another man? How many miscarriages she'd had without ever delivering a child?

We pay a high price when we cling to our dignity, when we seek to live freely in a society that denies us the right to live. It clothes us in hypocrisy and convinces us to be satisfied with so little. It denies our right to happiness. As we are sprinting down the fast track trying to make a living, we come up against the fact that we can hardly live off the few crumbs left there for us. They suffocated Auntie Samia because the man she loved was from a lower social class. The poor have no right to dream of change. Wiping the sweat from their brows, they have no right to dream. Even hopes and aspirations are confiscated from the oppressed to increase their desperation.

I mourned my auntie, the eyes she had kept closed, taking pride in refusing to be in love. I saw the eyes of her beloved, who'd married a woman of his own social class and remained the same—a wage worker who passed down that same crutch to his children, acquiescing to the socially accepted notion that the poor have no right to dream.

Hala had no rights. Her home was humble. She often struggled to light the fireplace to give her home some warmth and aspired to have central heating. But she was born poor and would take her destitution with her to the grave. She had no right to start a new family after her husband's corpse had turned to dust. That includes the baby she carries inside her even now.

My auntie made a big fuss and paid the price for her "no." She paid for it in lonely nights and extreme isolation, so she wouldn't be like all the women of our village who lock up love between their thighs, convinced that "living in the shadow of a wall is better than living in the shadow of a man." They claimed that even scarce shade is better than the sun. None of this mattered anymore now that she is dead. All I could do is stare at her body and think about how much like her I am. I only truly feel alive in Rabih's shadow. He is the lover whose shadow remains the sun that strips me naked.

But Auntie, don't Nabil and Rabih resemble each other? Aren't we mirrors of these men? Don't they also betray that great love that we women greedily grant free of charge—not to everyone but to some?

My auntie's passing showed me how much I'd changed. I was no longer the little girl waiting for everyone to be happy with her and pat her on the head. I looked at everything around me with coldness and contempt, as if my eyes existed only in that widening chasm between me and everything around me. I was someone who never connected to reality except through my ability to infiltrate it through my self-abnegation and sticking to preconceived identities that I no longer relate to. My husband's beatings stung my skin and aroused contradictions inside me: the first was out in the light of day, and submissive to him, the second was controlled by darkness and slapped him back without him knowing it.

Everything around me is phony. The women mourning my auntie had never visited her when she was lonely. The woman who washed her body had a heart of tin. She handled the corpse with professional care, seemingly unconcerned because my auntie wasn't actually there anymore. She acted as if, after death, a body turns into just a thing, a thing without a soul. But the body doesn't deteriorate into a lump of organs. The soul departs and leaves the body, to be messed with by the people who wash and shroud the dead. The woman who washed my auntie's body for no pay did so out of a desire for spiritual, not material, reward. For her, washing the dead was a dignified deed. Anyone who does this work knows firsthand the contours of life and death, awe and terror.

The soul gives the body its value and the body gives the soul a home through which to experience life. The body is what enables us to share everything with others: speaking, conversation, sight, touch, and tenderness. We are crystallized in its form and we reap what we sow within it. But in our societies where suppression seeps into our very pores, we learn to suppress our bodies for no other reason than to suppress our souls and separate the visible from the invisible. We are doubled beings because our bodies don't walk down the path of life with our souls. So as not to accumulate losses, we always need to keep one eye on the world and the other closed to it.

I had become separate from the reality I was no longer immersed in. I no longer bothered to wear makeup so he would think I was beautiful. I went into the bathroom and had a powerful desire to masturbate. I stretched out on the bathroom floor. My stomach pressed against the smooth, cool marble tiles. I conjured up Rabih in my mind, imagining our bodies close together. I saw myself the way I liked it: me lying on my back, him kissing the palms of my hands and then quickly moving on to put his head between my breasts. His fingers drew circles around my waist. I was completely relaxed and submissive, receiving his love and passion. I evoked Rabih's body and soul and took him inside me. I didn't feel emptiness; I would have sworn his ghost was with me. I stopped and went into Auntie Samia's bedroom.

I lay down on her bed, bringing my lover along with me. I felt that she was the only one who would understand my need for love. How couldn't she, when she crafted her Self out of passion, refusing to bring a man she would be forced to have intercourse with into her bed?

She tended to her garden lovingly. She planted her flowers with striking artistry and coordination. I enjoyed watching her compose the different color arrangements, putting a lot of green between them, saying, "Sweetie, you need to watch out for the flowers and help them breathe so they won't choke."

My auntie believed that we could see things better from a distance. You can see things with a different luster that way; if we touch them their details have a meaning. This is what set her apart and made her whole. It stemmed from her reconciliation with her Self, and her love for beauty, along with everything that comes alive and flows through life with elegance. She was so different from my mother, who was consumed by pain, a huge amount of which she passed down to me without even realizing it.

Sami called me because he knew I would be sleeping in the village until the mourning period was over. He tried to make his voice sound warm and friendly, but I sensed he was annoyed by my absence. I knew that he would take revenge on me for spending that night outside our marital bed, at the moment I least expected it. Perhaps it would be when my sorrow had begun to ease. I lay in bed thinking about my husband. I thought about him from a distance, as my auntie used to put it. Sami was irritated by everything that brought me joy. He always insisted on reminding me that he was the only source of joy in my life. The more I recollect my memories, the more I feel I don't deserve my feelings of guilt and humiliation, that I don't deserve anything good. Now I have lost this stupidity that haunted me for years; I know that man never loved me.

"Come here, Sahar, don't be afraid, come here."

I approached cautiously, taking small steps, a numbness in my bare feet. My hair hung in my face, my body heavy under the sheer nightshirt I was wearing. He told me to move faster. I stopped in front of him but didn't look at him. I looked down at the ground. He lifted the strands of hair hanging in my face. "Do you love me?" he asked. I was silent. "Are you upset because I hit you?"

I nodded. He grabbed me by the arm.

"Look at me," he demanded. "Why don't you love your husband? Your husband loves you."

I gathered up all my courage and replied, "Do you beat someone you love?"

He closed his eyes and clenched his teeth, like a saw trying to cut through an iron pipe. "You make me hit you. You get me so angry and just drive me crazy."

"What do I do?"

"You don't understand, you make me get so angry."

"Why? What do I do?"

He hit the edge of the bed with his hand, deliberately trying to frighten me. He asked me again, "Why don't you love Sami?"

I started to cry, which made him even angrier. He pushed his hair back, rose to his feet, and started pacing the room. "You don't love me," he repeated. "You don't understand, you make me so angry."

Through my tears, I searched my mind for any mistake I might have made. Why do I push him to rage? Am I that stupid? I sat down on the bed and buried my head in the pillow. Knowing that he was enraged and would soon want to have sex with me, I got more nervous and started feeling guilty. He joined me on the bed, lifted my head, and kissed me. "Do you love Sami?"

I nodded. And though I couldn't share his desire, I gave in to him so as not to make him lose his temper. After he finished, his expression seemed to indicate that he forgave me for making him angry. I didn't understand anything that was happening at that time. I was only watching him and myself. I didn't know why he treated me cruelly as a prelude to sex.

Why did he have to be so violent? Why did I spend so many years subject to his rage? If he fought with a colleague at work, he beat me. If he thought of how his mother dominated his father, he beat me too. If he wanted to prove that he was the handsomest man on the face of the earth, as his mother always said he was, he beat me even more. If he wanted to prove that he was different from his father who was controlled by his mother, then he was violent toward me.

He didn't like the way I made the bed. The food I prepared wasn't tasty, though he always wolfed it down. The clothes I wore were too revealing. Smoking wasn't appropriate for a woman. I wasn't very good at looking after my children and they surpassed me in their studies—not because I'd raised them well but because they inherited their intelligence and abilities from their father.

It wasn't fear that pushed me to surrender to his insults. It was to avoid problems. A woman surprised by everything happening around her without realizing it—that was me. Not afraid—I'd transcended that feeling. I was stunned, consumed by searching for an answer in him to everything that had happened between us. I was running from my own problems, trying to find the problems in him. After I'd been unfaithful to him, I discovered that I had been with him for so long that I'd forgotten myself. I forgot that I was a beautiful young woman, as if I'd made the premature decision to boycott my life and throw it in the trash bin. I'd accepted being Sami's mother, doll, and little prostitute, someone he liked to gaze at when she was naked and broken.

It's true that love requires no explanation. We just love. But because love means different things to different people, its description depends on the impulse behind it. Perhaps his love for me was obsessive. I was a drug for him, or simply debauchery that he could no longer do without. His jealous behavior reflected that he suffered from extreme possessiveness. His exaggerated suspicion stemmed from his inability to feel that he had caught me. In order to achieve this goal, he had to create the feeling in me that I always needed him. I'm not good at driving because I'm absent-minded; I can't make friends because no one but him loves me. This also meant that he strengthened his own bondage to me. After his bouts of madness passed, he once again made himself into the husband who seemed he might fulfill all my desires.

After beating me, he always cried and asked for my forgiveness. Even in his florid apologies, I saw nothing but the tears of a little boy afraid of losing a piece of candy. This is what helped allay my fear of him and made me realize that it was controllable if I consciously mastered and quashed the feeling that I needed him. In order to fight against this, I had to take back my stolen self. So I insisted on working, even if insurance was not the field in which I would find my self-realization and was quite distant from my repressed ambitions. But I had to break his feeling of ownership over me that he had calculated would hold me back.

CHAPTER 26

As I was doing my hair in front of the mirror, I realized how much I had changed. My features showed the passage of time; I looked tired, worn out. Death makes us more serene. Since the death of my aunt, I'd started to fade, as if everything had gone silent. I also realized that things inside me always happened quickly, so fast that I couldn't stop and think about them. I'd become short tempered. Tradition and life's humiliations had almost strangled my desires. My need to make love or to masturbate grew and grew. This is what I used to connect with that Other in my mind so I could find refuge, if only inside myself.

I did this less in search of an orgasm than out of a yearning for a sense of belonging. It was a way to belong to myself even if it was only a fantasy. Insomnia began to plague me, and Sami told me I was becoming unbearable. And like a woman living with a stranger, I suddenly stopped seeing him or even considering that he was there. I no longer listened when he spoke to me. I was totally absent, completely distracted. My Self was totally separate from me, and I found my body in the nothingness surrounding me while I was in another place. I no longer cared about events going on around me, as if my very existence no longer mattered. My rejection of fakeness, which spread like an epidemic through eerie silence, took shape.

When Sami approached me to have sex, I gave him my body with no resistance. I just endured it. There were no feelings. I was immersed in nothing, waiting for life to pass. He entered me and licked my breasts and I was totally numb. I didn't even want to fight him, not because I was giving in, but because I didn't want anything anymore, especially to wage pointless, morbid battles.

As much as that feeling of nothingness was comfortable, in that it erased the positive or negative results of specific situations, it also filled me with death. I ate mechanically and spoke without the slightest emotion. When I hid within my Self, I felt that I could no longer take hold of it. I lay in bed for hours, staring at the dim light from the courtyard coming in through the open window.

There was a white cover over the thin mattress, and the bedposts seemed to lean against each other. What had begun to haunt me was no ordinary sadness; feelings of bitterness overshadowed everything that might tempt me to rejoin life. I remembered Rabih's experience with the death of his parents and how he told me he felt that he was walking through life with no backbone. He said nothing satisfied him, and that having sex with prostitutes was a search for fleeting pleasure to feel convinced that he existed. But he was like a fugitive, fleeing in search of his mother's tender care, which his wife couldn't give him because of her domineering naivete. The prostitutes didn't provide him with this either, because they were just commodities he could buy. Thus he lost his essence, which connected him to the crack in his soul. Ultimately this left him feeling somewhat revolted rather than safe. I was a woman somewhere between these two. Through my passionate sexual appetite, I was always able to satiate his sensual side, and through my love, I was able to cultivate an atmosphere of tender care.

Rabih had many dreams to share with me, and he knew well that I was a dreamer too. He showed me how beautiful things could be if we had been together. He'd go into great detail about a bridge that we could use together to spy on a life that we never planned on building. This always made me feel hypersensitive and I would cry.

Now I am haunted by the absence of desire. I am barely able to move, almost paralyzed. Even the pleasure of cheating receded. In its place appeared sedimented traces of illusions. I was flooded with idealism, but this eventually collided with feelings of emptiness once again. Internalized rage and anger ate away at me as if the effects of accumulated years of distress were beginning to finally appear.

I recalled the story of my auntie Samia's only friend, Fadwa. She was the wife of an army officer called Assaf, who was arrested by the Syrian Mukhabarat in the mid-1980s and held for nearly a year. After he was released, Assaf came back to our village, where women showered him with rice and flowers; roses and lemon blossoms cascaded around him like a groom on his wedding day. "The hero has returned," everyone cheered. But, as his wife described it, Assaf did nothing to acknowledge the cheers. Instead, he searched longingly for her in the crowd. When their eyes finally met, she could tell that he was on the verge of tears. She was the only one who caught his gaze, and it felt as if she were both drowning in his eyes and looking out from within them.

"We sat down alone in our room, Samia. I came close to him and wanted to kiss him. He turned his head away. He had never, ever turned his face away from me before. Then he started to cry. He hid his face in his hands, sobbing like a little boy. I started crying too, but he kept his face turned away from mine, Samia. I don't know what the sons of bitches did to him. He didn't tell me. I asked him and he shook, but he didn't tell me. He couldn't move his lips—it was like they were stuck."

She told my auntie how her husband would wake up in the middle of the night shouting, "Leave me alone, get off me, you sons of bitches!" She would rush to wipe his forehead with a wet towel to calm his night terrors. He stayed like this for almost two months. She chose to keep quiet about the state he was in so as not to undermine his prestige in the village. One night, there was a strong wind blowing outside and Assaf was sitting near the window drinking mint tea.

"That night was amazing, unbelievable, it was like he had a rendezvous with the angels. He sat me down next to him and told me what they'd done to him. They beat him a lot, Samia. They tortured and humiliated him ... maybe they even raped him. Even now I don't know. I'll die not knowing."

Fadwa hugged her husband close, and he told her he didn't feel like the hero everyone kept saying he was. He felt insulted, violated, and bitter, that he had experienced the world's greatest evil and that his soul had no energy left. He locked himself in his house for two months, refusing to see anyone.

A bullet fired from his military weapon penetrated his brain one fateful night, leaving the house awash in blood. Fadwa cradled his bloody head in her lap. She first kissed the place where the bullet had entered his head, and then his face, even as her relatives circled around her, telling her, "Don't do that! Kissing the dead is haram."

"And what they did to Assaf isn't haram?" Fadwa cried out, loud enough to rouse her husband from his grave.

She too became paralyzed and haunted by disappointment. She tried to live a normal life but she couldn't. She spent many hours a day at Assaf's shrine. Whenever someone tried to convince her to stop visiting, her face turned bright red, her eyes bulged out, and she began to mutter incomprehensibly. But her contempt at this suggestion flared in her eyes and perhaps was enough explanation. On one of these nights, she even dozed off as she crouched next to the tombstone, her head resting on the cool marble.

Fadwa and my auntie shared bitterness and a perpetual fire in their bellies. This flame can't be seen, nor can the steam rising from their shared agonies. The first because her husband's rights had gone up in smoke, and his blood spilled out onto her body, dampening it so she couldn't staunch its flow. The second, because she was deprived of her right to love for untenable reasons and couldn't wage war for him. She hadn't agreed to elope with Nabil when he had asked her to, but she remained faithful to him and wove him into her imagination every day, living with his ghost.

Samia died, Assaf died and Fadwa soon passed away too, from an excess of sorrow. Like they once had, I began to see how death could be succor when you're drowning in a pool of degradation and insult. I felt bitter because of the years I endured beatings and silence. We believe this silence will save us or conceal our scars. But it tries to speak deep within us. It has an irrepressible desire to be freed; it is a wild horse whinnying and butting against our ribcage. There is no escape from where it's lodged inside us. I suffered as if all that bitterness were hanging off my internal organs, as if I'd tried to abort a fetus but it remained stuck at the opening of my uterus, and grew there, got bigger, and started kicking. My sorrow increased, and there was no way to control it by granting it a space of freedom through infidelity. Infidelity revealed things that had been hidden away in a cocoon. It revealed the outside world of love and the pleasures of the body. It became stronger than I was, as if life were colluding with my secret self. Whenever it crashed into death, it became a mirage. It piled up on top of me and I couldn't find it, but I kept looking at the curtains, which below back and forth over the window, depending on the direction of the wind. I was self-conscious; I also wanted to believe that there would be an end to this nothingness as with all things in life.

CHAPTER 27

The Other woman stood on a high up peak. She was not alone. Many men were there with her, including my father, my husband, and my lover. I half turned to look at her to see what she was doing, to let her know I was here, somewhere. She didn't see me. I kept staring at her, walking with an upright posture with those men so she could choose one of them. I wanted to know who she would choose, and then I saw her with a man I didn't know, walking calmly arm in arm with him. She slid down into the abyss and disappeared with him. Then I stood facing all those men. I tried to pass through them, but I couldn't. I called out to her, but I didn't know her name. I wanted to hug her close, to tell her everything about me and what I wanted—that I see myself alone, it doesn't matter where, anywhere, in the country or the city. I wanted to laugh with her or even just plunge into a long silence with her, gazing at the light in her eyes.

I remember the day I sat with Hala, who was daydreaming, somewhere far away. I asked her, "What are you thinking about?"

Hala was quiet for a moment and then replied, "When I was a girl, I only had one doll; you know we were very poor. I called her Farah. I named her Farah because this name means joy. When I dreamed about marrying Ahmad, I wanted to have a daughter we would call Farah, so I could give her all the things I wasn't allowed to have. Now I feel that all of my dreams have been dashed like the fruit of an imaginary tree that never blossoms."

"At least you haven't stopped dreaming, Hala. I don't even know if I'm alive."

"What use are dreams if they don't come true?"

"They numb our reality and help us accept it, because they can perhaps foretell better days."

"But like joy, Farah is a mirage."

"Who said that you can't have children?"

"That? No, never… I am afraid."

"But you said that nothing frightens you."

"I think that I lie a lot."

"We all do."

"We are all illusions."

"Why don't you try to look for her? Somewhere inside yourself?"

"Who?"

"Farah."

"I fear she'll never come."

"Have you made space for her arrival?"

"No, not really. I am like you my friend. I've lost faith in life."

"That's what Other people want from you, Hala—for you to turn into a plaything because you lost your virginity and your husband. They try to sever our faith in new beginnings. Weren't you set on transforming your living room into an institute to teach English?"

"Yes, I was."

"Why didn't you do it then?"

"I am trying. It's something that takes a lot of effort."

"Try! What have you got to lose? Maybe then Farah will come later."

"And if she doesn't come?"

"She will, and she'll have a big rear end like yours!"

"I don't want her to."

Hala was silent for a moment, then responded, "Sahar, what if Farah doesn't come?"

"She will come; don't get ahead of yourself. Don't begin from the end."

"And if she doesn't?"

"There is no doubt in my mind that she will, my friend."

Hala was quiet for a minute, pondering how her whole life had seeped into her features—all the sorrow that she denied, all the disappointments that crashed down around her, all the mayhem that she carried inside her. She only wanted Farah: the joyful little girl who could never be, a girl whose mother would love her, care for her, make her happy, and give her the motivation, safety, and hope needed to propel her toward her dreams. Farah was what Hala both renounced and longed for—a family, warmth, and love. None of her lovers ever paid her enough attention or tried to get through to her. They made her into what they needed. She feigned strength, but actually experienced the most vicious kind of weakness—the hidden kind that doesn't even know itself. Her lovers were happy because they'd slept with a beautiful woman without even having to make an effort. They didn't care to discover what was hidden inside of her. If they could have savaged every part of her, they wouldn't have refused.

What did Hala do but harm herself in order to announce that she had the right to live life?

I didn't discover the extent of Hala's fragility until I saw her sitting in the corner of her room when her son's diabetes had taken a turn for the worse and she wasn't able to pay for his medication. Her plight had stripped her of her independence, and she realized that she wanted more from a man than a quick, dull meeting of bodies. She wanted a man who made her feel he was her partner, but perhaps she didn't even want that anymore. My friend was one of those women who left themselves open to life, so men thought she was available. Because they felt this, she accepted her fate as revenge against them.

She propped herself up against the wall and rocked her upper body back and forth. She started crying, spitting, and screaming. She struck her face and then punched the wall. I tried to hug her, but she shouted brutally, "No one gets close to me. Get the hell away from me."

She dug her nails into her own flesh that she drew blood, and then let out a moan, cursing God and everything in his creation. Suddenly her entire body was shaking and quivering, as if gasping for her last breath. She seemed to embody the apex of human suffering, in the form of a woman cast out by the world and forbidden to improve herself. She began scratching her cheeks and wounding her face, repeating, "Is this good? How about this?"

Little by little, she stopped harming herself as her strength ran out, and finally collapsed to the floor shivering. Lying on her left side with bent knees, she began running her right hand up and down her arm, patting her body, as if apologizing for the beating. She realized how pathetic she was, how those men had messed with her and sucked everything out of her. Hala's suffering became palpable to me, even as my own sorrows refused to leave me and I felt nothingness once again.

As I looked at her I thought about her torments, which she resisted in her contempt for everything at the very beginning. Can a woman who voluntarily surrenders herself to a group of men feel abused? She resembled Rabih so much—the way he threw himself into the arms of prostitutes to buy and sell both himself and them.

Hala used to say that she'd spent half her life cleaning up after other people, and that she didn't intend to spend her remaining years doing it. Rabih also considered himself to have been exploited by everyone, and those dark feelings pricked at him. They both chose absurdity but found no comfort in it. This afforded them a few minutes of reassurance, but then it would slip in suddenly and show them their spirits' ruin. This is an eternal maxim: the victim becomes the executioner. The executioner breaks down, hearing the sound of the whip slashing into someone else's body boomeranging back to him, reminding him of the whip that flogged him. Life is a vicious circle—the end is the beginning and the beginning the end. He wonders if he knew life, or what we turn into without realizing it.

Hala was bigger than this, but no one wanted to believe her. She was better than quick sex and just leaving. She was better than her lovers' accusations of immorality or her belief that she didn't deserve to be Farah's mother, just because she gave them her body. They didn't know that for Hala, Farah was far superior, something they wouldn't be able to implant in her womb. Hala's faith in Farah pushed her to leave every time. No one actually cared if Farah came, despite seeming to hope that she would.

She discovered men through sex and when she realized how meaningless their bodies were to her, she would rush to leave, for fear that Farah's father would be a bad man like her own father.

CHAPTER 28

Hala became tougher over time, striving to assert herself to compensate for the loss of her family and loved ones, and even her feeling of not belonging to the nation. Hala spoke with unfamiliar sensuality, but not about sex, rather as a different way to prove her existence. Her small body rose and fell, deliberately trying to evoke lust in men.

Hala told me that she'd searched for her brother Ibrahim for nearly a year, and that one of the preachers told her that he'd died in Iraq. I asked her why she'd hidden this from me for all this time. She replied that she'd refused to believe it. She kept hoping that her brother would come back one day. I knew that Hala didn't lie, though she kept many things around her in the shadows. Other things, she hid for a while, but revealed them later. Why am I surprised by what she said then? Didn't my aunt's death awaken me from being plunged into nothingness, betrayal, and chasing after a mirage? Hala was in a constant struggle with life, and she struggled with only one being—herself. I too used to struggle with silence and the fear of being more vocal about my existence. Her dark, honey-colored eyes harbored anxiety and the fear of ending up alone, torn apart and unbalanced.

As Hala talked excitedly, she reached into her purse and took out some colored ribbons and pieces of paper cut into different shapes and sizes.

"I am going to call it the Farah Institute, and start with one small room in my house, specifically the room where I used to unfold a mattress every night and sleep. The house will become so much nicer. I've saved a bit of money. I plan to decorate it and give lessons to the neighborhood kids when I finish working at the company. My son can be with me. See? My plan is almost complete."

At that moment, Hala seemed almost like Farah, the daughter she didn't know if she would ever give birth to but whom she'd tried to create. She didn't want to be wealthy or even rich. She didn't want to be the harsh, cold woman who didn't know love. She tried many times and she succeeded in a number of intermittent, unreal periods, like a full tree that only bears the fruits of illusion, leaving bits of its body and soul on the bodies of lovers like branches carrying the autumn upon them. When I looked at her, I remembered her in her worst crises and in the most desperate stages of her life, when she reckoned that the light shining in her eyes would never see the sun again. All of that ran in opposite directions, fear and deprivation seemed insignificant faced with a serious attempt to confront life and find a little joy.

I always wanted to be Farah, that joy. I looked forward to being able to resist stubbornly, without being an enemy to myself. I observed my eyes' enigmatic plea in the mirror to tempt her to unite with me in an attempt to embrace life, even in old age.

When I was lying near my husband, I used to feel my body automatically resist, like a person who didn't want to get ready to sleep, but simply to leave—for somewhere far or near, low or high, no difference, just somewhere else. If Hala had caught the first notion of a dream from a bitter experience, I feared that I was nothing more than a black hole. I repeatedly thought about my friend who, after a long struggle, had hit the road, not knowing her chances of failure or success.

I gathered up the leaves of my life as if stealthily running naked on tiptoes, bending to pick up what remained of them without losing the thrill of facing up to what I'd been trying to escape since I was born. I forced myself to sit with Hala, and made myself small so she would open up to me, far from anyone else, far from Rabih.

When I felt obsessive, I feared becoming like that piece of fruit about to fall off of a tree, only to be left alone to rot because no one would picked it up. I automatically lost my desire when I was far from Rabih. I was condemned to fear. I was terrified whenever I was alone with myself even for a short period. I asked myself: who had the answers to my life's questions, who was in charge? Why did I veer from experiencing joy to extreme sadness? What is the path to salvation?

I was like a chess player who suffered repeated defeats but understood that the next move would make up for the past. A number of times I thought about killing myself because I felt it was impossible to attain a reality so distant from the one I lived. I thought a lot about Hala and envied her for her ability to work through her bitterness or convince herself that she could. I imagined her when she was young amidst the noise and filth in that neighborhood she grew up in, with its ugly apartment buildings and pyramids of garbage piled up on the banks of the Abu Ali river, for nobody knew how long.

Many times, I asked myself what I could do to help her or mitigate that vague harm that she had never given me a complete picture of. The sad truth was that no one could help Hala because no one would ever know what had happened to her during those years of accumulated oppression. She never told me all of the details, but it seemed to me that if I had pressed her, she would have pulled one terrible story after another about the depravity of the human soul out of her sleeve.

Deep down, I knew she was much more afraid of suffering than she had spoken about. When she said, "No one knows how much blood actually costs," I knew she had experienced the bitterness of death. But she always arose from beneath the rubble, digging her fingernails into her skin, because she was determined to dance even in the face of death—just as free people dance in their prison cells.

I never knew the cost of the victory that she swore to herself she would achieve. I asked myself what force drove her to hope, what allowed her to smell like a pleasant fragrance that grew stronger when she laughed, revealing the tiny blue veins under her skin.

She embodied the living, breathing youth of the village, without inhibitions or secret calculations, with a big dose of naivete, and the will to live day to day, outside of customs and norms. I gradually saw how she managed to overcome her inner struggles by quickly adapting, and not letting a single dark idea paralyze her.

She stunned me by talking about that fuzzy idealism that she had paid so dearly for. Perhaps maintaining her dignity and free will is what pushed her to embrace life, while I wallowed about somewhere between regret and fear. I remained thirsty for that stillness that I'd only experienced a few times during my self-imposed seclusion.

But my years of abuse transformed me into a mere thing, shackled to its owner like a slave girl perhaps, or a dog. Because I accepted being treated his way, I was nearly certain that I would end up crazy or dead. Was it some kind of masochistic impulse that pushed me toward this torture, because I knew that if I acted irrationally, I would suffer a lot and that I was safe when I was being humiliated?

While Hala was hurtling toward her dream, doing everything she could to make it come true, I was taking sedatives that only made me feel blank and submerged in silence. In this quiet of mine, I was like my city, mired in filth, waiting to see what could be salvaged from within its ruins. All of the deprivation in its displaced neighborhoods, and the cumulative encroachments on them, which plunge it into a deep slumber, make it vulnerable to all manner of misery and sorrow. Like me, it is unable to rise up from under the oppressive pollution to find some kind of light or hope flickering on the horizon.

As I grew increasingly silent, my husband's rage intensified. He started having screaming fits that were like him thrashing me with a loud whip. I lost all feeling both in my body and in my dreams. All I kept thinking about was the saying, "It's better late than never." But on one of those nights of somber darkness, I was struck by a strong desire to waste that body, which could not contain its beauty. So, searching for some silence, I swallowed all of my sedatives at once.

But death—that being that had so injured me—didn't take me. It left me hanging, attached to machines in the hospital where they pumped my disturbed stomach. Powerless and frail, I had been ready to put an end to my life. That is what broke my Self that everyone around me, one after another, had created out of their own tragedies. Their faces and bodies gathered around me in the cramped hospital room.

My mother cried for the first time. My father frantically paced the hospital corridors. I heard the voices of Sami and his parents engaged in an argument outside. Hala was shouting at them venomously, laying blame on every creature present.

Images of each of them passed through my mind, one by one: my lover who did not acknowledge my existence publicly. Hala's voice saying, "I leave them before they can leave me." My auntie Samia, whispering to me, "We humans betray ourselves." Sami, who betrayed his need for compassion with his obstinacy. Rabih, betraying his picture; Hanadi, her past. Dunya asking me, "Mama, what does unfaithful mean?" And Hala's son who claimed he wasn't sick to defy his horrid fate.

When they came in to check on me, waves of panic washed over me and I wanted to shout: "He's called Ernesto Che Guevara, Mama! The Soviet Union collapsed, Dad. We aren't a perfect family. We aren't even a happy family … we're miserable. I want to live. I don't want to live as little as possible, but more than all this. I want to feel alive. I'm tired of your cold walls. Don't you see how wretched we are? When did you hear music? I want to feel joy. Am I asking too much? I just want some tranquility and reassurance. I want you all out of me. I want to be me. I want to be a divorced woman. I don't want a man to beat me. I want to open my spirit to a new tomorrow full of sunshine and hope."

They took me to the emergency room. I was in the hospital for an entire week, denied all visitors. The doctor came to speak to me and I babbled incomprehensibly that Hala's brother was a fundamentalist and that the people who taught him about jihad are the same ones who sow a culture of fear in our city. I informed him that my husband hurt me openly and I hurt him secretly. I spoke to him at length about Rabih's quick rise to affluence and his obsession with poverty.

They injected me with many needles and a tingling feeling spread through my body. I was told that I needed to go abroad to recover. In the sanctuary that I was in, I asked every day for Sami to be kept away. I told them that I wasn't the Sahar who they knew, that another woman was inhabiting me and she seemed determined to stay there. Sami's family shamed him for having a crazy wife, who wasn't good for anything, and urged him to be rid of me.

My parents were extremely empathetic, like people atoning for their sins. Even my atheist father started asking God to restore my health. He realized that his daughter, who had grown apart from him just as his desire to find justice waned, urgently needed him. My mother hugged Tareq and Dunya with so much tenderness, in a way she had never held me, and asked if she could take them with her and care for them, far from my husband, until I recovered.

At dawn, just as the first rays of sunlight appeared, I stood at the Beirut International Airport holding two suitcases. As the customs agent was about to stamp my passport, I looked at him pleadingly and said, "Please don't."

"Are you sure, Mme. Sahar?" he asked.

"Sir," I said, "there has been some confusion. I am called Hala and I don't want to leave. I have a daughter called Farah waiting for me."

TRANSLATOR'S NOTE

The process of translating *All the Women Inside Me* was not easy. From the pithy three-word Arabic title and trying to choose an English title to approximate it, to debating finer points of long sentences in the final edits, the complexities of this book were difficult to render in translation. One reason for this is that *All the Women Inside Me* is not an easy book. The novel is a searingly intense psychological portrait of Sahar. A woman trying to escape physical and emotional abuse in her family, she lives under first her parents' and then her husband's control in her hometown of Tripoli, North Lebanon. Sahar is constantly stifled and stymied by life's many challenges and finds an escape within her own imagination, and by engaging the women and men who inhabit it.

The non-linear, meandering style and structure of the book mirror what happens within Sahar's mind. The most difficult part of rendering this text in translation is to balance the need to capture this style with the shorter, less descriptive and metaphor-laden sentences favored in English prose. On the other hand, at times extremely concise Arabic phrases often need many words in English to make sense.

The compact Arabic title, *Ana wa-Hiya wa'l-Okhrayat*, cannot be captured in English. What we settled on, after many conversations between publisher, author, and translator, is not as powerful. It is not a direct translation of the Arabic words either—a literal translation of the title is "Me, and She, and the Other Women." I wanted to capture some of the meaning and also make the title something that alluded directly to Elhassan's original title. I also wanted the English title to evoke the multiple lives and selves that Sahar experiences throughout the book, especially at the end. It was also important to me for the title to invoke the notion of many women, multiple women.

Another element of the original Arabic novel that goes missing in translation is the protagonist's name. Sahar is an Arabic name for a woman, meaning the time of day just before dawn. But the three-letter root system of Arabic means that words also carry meanings related to other words of the same root. Thus, the name Sahar also recalls words like captivate, charm, enchant, enthrall, bewitch, and mesmerize, among others. In English, the name does not have a meaning at all, let alone allusive and layered meanings such as these. The same is true for the name of the girl who becomes so important towards the end of the book, Farah. If you replace the word Farah with its literal meaning, Joy, you will begin to see the layers of meaning.

Another difficult element of translating this novel was that it is not plot-driven, and so the accuracy of conveying action or describing content was not the focus. Instead, I was compelled to think about how to replicate or at least convey the author's ample use of metaphors and allusion, as well as the exploration of Sahar's rich interior life. At times in the original Arabic, this is difficult to follow and can even be confusing, albeit intentionally.

The narration is meant to be linear, and at certain points it only happens within Sahar's imagination. This is described sometimes directly; at others it is alluded to, or told, indirectly. All of this is challenging to the reader on many levels, in the Arabic original and all the more so when it is one step removed, in English translation.

A line from the *New York Times* review of my translation of Jana Elhassan's other novel, *The Ninety-Ninth Floor*, has haunted me since I read it. The reviewer confidently asserts that, "it's the political rather than the personal that's most engaging for the foreign reader" [Allison McCollough, "Fiction in Translation" *New York Times* February 17, 2017]. And while I would not dispute that there are many interesting explorations of politics in this book, it is in fact the social and even more so the personal and intimate that is, in my opinion, the most engaging feature of the book. I would posit that this would be true for any reader of *The Ninety-Ninth Floor*—"foreign" or not. And if this is true of Elhassan's earlier novel, it is all the truer of *All the Women Inside Me*.

Who is the English reader and what are they most interested in reading about in translation? What kinds of compromises must a translator make when helping a text move from Arabic into English that is not "about" difference? The book's protagonist and most of its characters are Muslims, but it is not *about* Islam. The text is set in the northern Lebanese city of Tripoli and describes some of its spaces in great detail, but it is not *about* Tripoli or life there either. The novel's very close attention to detail in describing Tripoli, and the middle-class lives of its Muslim characters, both adds to its specificity but also under-lines its universality. It is the story of women struggling to break free of male control, from a patriarchy not only found where it is set, but all over the world. The abuse Sahar suffers and eventually flees is not one unique to Islam, Muslims, Tripoli, Lebanon, and so on, but recognizable to people globally. The brilliance of Elhassan's writing is to capture something very particular about this one fictional woman, and her friends, family, and milieu, and in so doing tell us something about ourselves as well.

What draws the reader to *All the Women Inside Me* and what will keep them in the text therefore is the intensity of the portrait of Sahar: her life, her imagination, her feelings. Readers have told me how real the struggles Sahar faces are and how genuinely they can relate to what she is describing, even as so much of what is contained in the book is Sahar describing her own imaginary world. I hope that this translation is successful in bringing Sahar, her imagination, and her world to people in the English language and in so doing have captured some—though certainly not all—of the beauty of the original Arabic novel.

TRANSLATOR'S ACKNOWLEDGMENTS

The work of translation is challenging, creative work and it is a pleasure to work with an author as an open conversation partner, so my first and most important thanks are due to Jana Elhassan. I would also like to draw attention to the work of Michel Moushabeck and the team at Interlink Publishing who remain committed to producing high quality translations—especially of Arabic literature—through the difficult times of the Covid-19 pandemic.

This short, compelling novel was translated in a series of long binge-like sessions and took many revisions, most of which were done during the global pandemic. I would like to thank my two research assistants who aided me with this translation through many discussions, individually and together: Sarah Abdelshamy and Caline Nasrallah. I appreciate their care and thought about how to make it as engaging as possible in English. And for their focus group-style help—always on call for questions—thanks to Alison Slattery, Farah Khan, Amanda and Tameem Hartman.

This translation is dedicated to all the women, wherever they are, who yearn to and try to leave, whether they manage to or not.